Praise for

HUNGER

★"If ever there was a book primed to show American children why families from other countries are often desperate to reach our shores, this is it." —*Booklist*, starred review, on the audio edition

★"The first-person narrative portrays Lorraine's family and community with realistically drawn personalities and relationships as well as fine-tuned ethical dilemmas, while sketching in the backdrop of the wider catastrophe. A moving personal story."

—*Booklist*, starred review

"Napoli skillfully evokes Lorraine's close-knit community, interweaving elements of Irish culture, history, and land- and seascape in ways that make the story accessible and appealing. Lorraine's affection for her family and solidarity with her starving friends deepen the sense of personal tragedy endemic to this terrible era. In an appended author's note, Napoli emphasizes the courage it takes for refugees to leave a country in crisis, and the courage it takes for those who choose to stay—a timely reminder about conditions in our current world."

—*Horn Book*

"The Irish people of the time are portrayed as stoic, strong, and proud, but also as victims of the wealthy, ruling British class. The ending may leave some readers wondering about the characters' choices and perhaps disagree with them, which could foster lively discussions."

—*School Library Journal*

ALSO BY DONNA JO NAPOLI

Hush

Hidden

Storm

Bound

Beast

Breath

HUNGER

A Tale of Courage

DONNA JO NAPOLI

A Paula Wiseman Book

SIMON & SCHUSTER BFYR

NEW YORK LONDON TORONTO SYDNEY NEW DELHI

An imprint of Simon & Schuster Children's Publishing Division
1230 Avenue of the Americas, New York, New York 10020

Text copyright © 2018 by Donna Jo Napoli
Cover photo and composite by Laurent Linn; photograph of hands holding soil copyright © 2018 by Compassionate Eye Foundation/Steven Errico/Getty Images

For information about special discounts for bulk purchases, please contact Simon & Schuster Special Sales at 1-866-506-1949 or business@simonandschuster.com.
The Simon & Schuster Speakers Bureau can bring authors to your live event. For more information or to book an event, contact the Simon & Schuster Speakers Bureau at 1-866-248-3049 or visit our website at www.simonspeakers.com.
Also available in a SIMON & SCHUSTER BFYR hardcover edition
Cover design by Laurent Linn
Interior design by Hilary Zarycky
Map art by Ryan Thompson
The text for this book was set in Adobe Caslon Pro.
Manufactured in the United States of America
First SIMON & SCHUSTER BFYR paperback edition June 2019
2 4 6 8 10 9 7 5 3 1
The Library of Congress has cataloged the hardcover edition as follows:
Names: Napoli, Donna Jo, 1948– author.
Title: Hunger / Donna Jo Napoli.
Description: First Edition. | New York : Simon & Schuster Books for Young Readers, [2018] | A Paula Wiseman Book. | Summary: In the autumn of 1846 in Ireland, twelve-year-old Lorraine and her family struggle to survive during the Irish potato famine, but when Lorraine meets Miss Susanna, the daugher of the wealthy English landowner who owns Lorraine's family's farm, they form an unlikely friendship that they must keep secret due to the deep cultural divide between their two families.
Identifiers: LCCN 2017015620 | ISBN 9781481477499 (hardback) | ISBN 9781481477512 (eBook) | ISBN 9781481477505 (pbk)
Subjects: LCSH: Ireland—History—Famine, 1845–1852—Juvenile fiction. | CYAC: Ireland—History—Famine, 1845–1852—Fiction. | Famines—Ireland—Fiction. | Survival—Fiction. | Friendship—Fiction.
Classification: LCC PZ7.N15 Hu 2018 | DDC [Fic]—dc23
LC record available at https://lccn.loc.gov/2017015620

To Rachel and Lorraine,
who, one way or another,
brought me to Ireland

ACKNOWLEDGMENTS

With much gratitude to Barry Furrow and Sam Charney, Laurie Garry, Alice Lamotta, Maureen Murray, Jenica Nasworthy, Jeannie Ng, Colleen O'Brien, Melinda Rahm, Carol Rendleman, Aida Ruan, Leyna Sweger, and Katharine Wiencke for comments on earlier drafts. And a giant thank-you to Trinity College Dublin for giving me a Long Room Hub Visiting Fellowship in 2012, so I could do the research foundational to this story. But most of all, a thousand thanks go to Paula Wiseman, without whom this book would never have been written and whose patience and gentle prodding helped to shape both my thinking and my words.

BEFORE YOU BEGIN

In August 1845, *Phytophthora infestans*—a fungus-like organism—attacked the potato crop in Ireland. Since potatoes are nutritious and packed with calories, and since they grow easily even in rocky soil, they were the mainstay of the diet of ordinary workers, including farmers. The potato blight led to a dramatic crop failure and widespread hunger throughout the country. Rural people in particular suffered. But no one was spared.

This story begins the following August.

Part 1

Sliding into Autumn, 1846

CHAPTER ONE

Green

We crested the hill and Da stopped. He slid his bulging sack on the ground, wiped his big palm down his mouth, and put his fists on his hips. The stony bunching in his cheeks that had been building up as we approached the top now melted smooth. The thumping of my heart suspended. *Please please let it be good news.* Da jerked his chin toward the fields below.

Oh, thank the heavens.

I swallowed, turned my head from Da, and dared to look down. Green. Green green green. As green as it had been this morning when we'd left here—a fond farewell—and now an even fonder welcome back in late afternoon. Lush Irish green, as Granny used to say. She said the green of forests like the one we stood in now and the green of pastures beside the long, long road going north and south—the road I'd traveled only into town, but never beyond—that green helped her not to grieve the green of the sea way past that field to the west. The green she'd grown up with, but was too far from to see once she'd come to live with us. Ireland was green everywhere. And, best of all in this moment, the field below was green.

That field was healthy. Our spud field was still healthy!

Each day we worried anew, and each day it had stayed green. With any kind of luck, we'd have a good harvest this year. In another month, no more growling bellies. We'd be eating our fill.

Yes, it had been a grand Sunday after all, despite my initial disappointment. I had yearned to spend the day playing with the other children after church. But for the past two weeks, I'd had extra chores on Sunday, so it was pure stubbornness that made me allow myself to hope for a reprieve. Da was always finding new ways to earn a bit of money and lately he'd decided to pull me along. Today he'd even brought little Paddy. It was good, though, in the end it was good, because so long as the field stayed green, life would get better again. We kids would have plenty of Sundays to play.

"Look, Paddy," I said, pointing to the Aran Islands, which were way off in the bay near Galways. This was the only point around here where you could get such a view. The islands were flat on top, as though the sea winds had worn them down. I imagined I could hear the wind blowing across those rocks— whistling secrets, howling sorrows.

"That's where I lived as a boy. On the one called Inis Mór." Da put his hand on top of little Paddy's head. We both knew this, of course, but we nodded reverently all the same. "If you look hard, you can see the Cliffs of Moher beyond."

Obediently, we stared southward. I'd never caught a glimpse of the cliffs before, and today was no exception.

"See? See that plume of spray there? That one, there? That's the sea crashing against the cliffs."

I leaned forward and concentrated. Sometimes I wondered if anyone could really see the spray or even the cliffs from here. But I didn't question Da. He was proud of the fact that he'd visited those cliffs once upon a time. Maybe his pride gave him better vision.

I was proud too. Proud of being a daughter of this green land. I squeezed little Paddy's hand in happiness, then dropped it and ran.

Rocks skittered out from under my bare feet. But I was deft; I wouldn't go tumbling with them. It was heavy today, a dead day, the air wet from held-in rain for the third day in a row. I knew the temperature was low. But in the shimmer of all that green below, the day seemed absurdly and deliciously warm. The wind born from my own running cooled me in the loveliest way. I opened my mouth wide, to gulp the world.

"Owwww!"

Of course. I stopped and closed my eyes for a second—it didn't serve anyone to show my annoyance—then went back and helped little Paddy up to sitting. Blood ran from a gash in his shin. Pebbles embedded there.

"Clean him up." Da strode on past with a quick glance and playful tug at my hair. "Bold girl. Your ma's going to be cross. You know your brother's clumsy."

"It's not my fault! I didn't tell him to run."

"You ran," Da said, not bothering to stop. "What did you think he would do? You're bold, not thick. My strong, bold girl." The sack of peat thumped on his back, but in a bouncy way, so I was sure he wasn't cross, at least. He'd sell nearly all that peat in town—so that was good. And, most of all, no one could be cross so long as the field was green.

I looked around. The path here was lined with the occasional milkwort. I ripped off a stem and handed it to little Paddy. "Chew on this while I go find something to clean you up with."

"Will it make it hurt less?"

I didn't know about that. New mothers used milkwort to make their milk flow better. But I didn't think little Paddy needed to hear that. I shrugged. "It might taste good."

I scooted off through the brush and searched. The grasses here in this little stony meadow should have been stiff and rough this time of year. They should have scratched me raw. Instead, the few plants were soft, as though the earth was holding on to whatever wet it could. As I went farther, they got denser. A thin creek trickled along, making a whisper of a song. I hadn't known it was there. I didn't know these hills well. We children hardly ever wandered this far. It was only because of gathering the peat on the other side that we'd gone today. How sweet that stream made everything—not just the grasses, the air itself.

Peppermint grew along the stream's edge. That was good for calming nausea, at least. And here were some lavender plants. Lavender was good for fending off pesky insects, like mosquitoes. I broke off some of each and dragged them through the creek water to get them clean. Oh. Oh, glory! Blackberry brambles hung over the water on the other side of the stream. They arced like huge, tangled claws of a devil monster, and they were laden with fruit. My stomach clenched in hunger.

I looked around. Nothing to carry them in.

I pulled my dress off over my head. I was really too old to go without clothes, and Ma would be beyond cross when I got home. But no one was likely to see me between now and then, so what did it matter? I picked as many berries as my dress could hold and hurried back to little Paddy with the precious parcel.

He sat on the path in the same spot, but with one hand high in the air now. He flapped it at me, nothing more than a movement of the wrist, but I recognized it as a warning. His eyes were big and he slowly turned his head to look from me to something at his other side. I stepped softly toward him, half alarmed.

A huge blue underwing moth crawled along little Paddy's outstretched leg. It was big as a bat. Dusk was still at least an hour off; that moth shouldn't have been out and about yet. I hardly breathed as I set down my parcel. I peeled open the sides and took out two blackberries. I placed them on my tongue and shut my mouth, careful not to crush them. Then I got on all fours and crept the rest of the way to little Paddy. The moth paid me no attention. I took a berry from my tongue and extended my hand, slowly, slowly, and put the berry on little Paddy's leg, in the moth's path. I took the other berry and put it in little Paddy's open mouth.

"*Blasta*—tasty," he said softly.

The moth touched the blackberry tentatively with feather-like antennae. All at once his silver-gray wings shot open, exposing the glorious lilac blue beneath. Little Paddy reached out his hand to pet it, and the moth flew. My heart fell. But the moth circled and landed back again, on little Paddy's head. Little Paddy laughed and the moth flew again. Away now.

"He was blue like smoke."

"Mmm," I said. I plucked the blackberry from little Paddy's leg and ate it.

"Blackberries are so good," said Paddy.

"They are, aren't they?"

"Lorraine?"

"What, Paddy?"

"I'm sorry I got you in trouble."

"Da wasn't really cross."

"He sounded cross."

"Watch the set of his shoulders, the way he walks—they give him away." I filled little Paddy's hand with blackberries. "He's happy really." I almost added that Da would be happy so long as the fields were green and the spuds were coming, but I caught myself in time. Who knew what little Paddy understood at his age? "Look out to the side and suck on your berries. And if it hurts a lot, sing with me."

Little Paddy put a berry in his mouth and dutifully stared to his side.

"On the wings of the wind," I sang, as I picked each pebble from his gash, *"o'er the dark rolling deep, angels are coming to watch o'er thy sleep."*

"I'm not going to sleep," said little Paddy. "And that hurts a lot. Besides, you sing all ugly."

"Just sing with me, you hear?"

"Angels are coming to watch over thee," we sang, *"so list to the wind coming over the sea."*

I rubbed the wound clean with the wet lavender. Then the peppermint.

"That's not making it feel better."

"But it makes you smell better." I laughed. "You're like some English lady's garden now, hidden on the other side of a wall, but fragrant for all."

"I'm cold."

So was I all of a sudden. The weather had been like this lately, warmer in the day, sometimes nearly hot, then shivery at night. I wished I could put my dress back on. "The sun's going down. We can't dodder."

"It's getting fierce. Carry me."

"I've got the berries to carry."

"I'll carry the berries. You carry me. Please, Lorraine."

I closed up the parcel and handed it to him. "Don't squish them, you hear?"

"I used to carry eggs all the time. When we still had hens."

"Berries ruin far easier than eggs." I turned and bent my knees.

Little Paddy climbed onto my back. Then he perched the parcel on top of my head.

"Don't be thick, Paddy. It'll fall off."

"I'll hold it there. Like the moth."

That made no sense. But lots of things little Paddy said didn't make sense. I tramped along down the hill.

"Let's pretend it's spud-planting time again, Lorraine. You know, let's chant the rules like we did then."

So spuds were on his mind too. I hoped he was just remembering our spring—not really worrying. I worried enough for both of us. "Smash those seashells," I said.

"Smash! Smash! Smash!" Little Paddy wriggled on my back. I thought about him swinging the hammer in March. He was better at it this year. Most of the shells were reduced to grit. "Ready!" he shouted.

"Add water to the pig manure. Three parts water, one part manure."

"Stir! Stir! Stir!" shouted Little Paddy. He was practically bouncing on my back, and well he should be. That manure gave the mixture exactly the nutrients spuds needed.

"Now add the smashed shells," I said.

"Dump! Dump! Dump!" shouted little Paddy. "Stir! Stir! Stir!"

"It's time," I said. "Mind the line."

"The line! The line!" he shouted.

I marched very straight as though I was following one of the long lines Da made in the field with the spade. "Throw it!" I said.

"There! There! There!"

I felt his little body twist, and I knew he was pretending to throw handfuls of the crushed seashells and manure mix onto the grass on either side of the spade line. I grasped his legs tighter. "Throw it thick," I chanted.

"There! There! There!"

"Turn the sod," I chanted.

"Turn! Turn! Turn!"

Little Paddy hadn't really ever helped with this part of the spud planting. But he had stood beside us this spring as Da and I did it. I remembered how my arms ached at the end of the day, how my back and neck and legs ached. Turning the sod over onto the mix of manure and shells was the hardest work ever. Harder even than digging for spuds in the autumn.

"Now, see how that turned-over sod makes such a lovely incubator for the seed spuds? It's grand!"

"Grand!" shouted little Paddy.

"You're a good help, Paddy. The best. So you can have the best treat of all. You get to put in the seed spuds."

"Hurrah!" shouted little Paddy. "Shove! Shove! Shove!"

I remembered his skinny arms pushing those little spuds into place. I remembered all our hopes as the pile of seed spuds gradually disappeared.

I marched ever more happily now, the rest of the way down the hill and past the fields, all the way home to our stone cottage. A wiggly brother on my back, and a green, green world. What could be better?

CHAPTER TWO

Pointy

I want more."

"Is that so, Paddy?" said Ma. "And exactly whose plate are you planning on robbing them from, you little *gadaí—* thief?"

Little Paddy twisted his mouth.

Ma was right, of course. Still, I understood little Paddy; the mound of blackberries didn't look nearly so large divided into our four cups as it had piled up in my dress, especially since Ma had given Da double what the rest of us got. I just bet his berries would fill two hen's eggshells with some left over. I stared at them till my eyes burned.

"Hmm. Thinking about it now, I wonder if maybe I did make a mistake," said Ma. "If a person had some blackberries before coming to the table, then that amount should be subtracted from his share, right?"

Little Paddy pressed his lips together and looked down. "I didn't." He shook his head. "Neither did Lorraine," he mumbled.

That my brother could fib so easy never surprised me. What surprised me was that he did it so bad. His cheeks flamed bright in the pale light from the peat fire in the hearth. The pungent reek was so comforting, though, who could get cross?

And Ma didn't. She just laughed. "That's settled, then. Lorraine, go get your da."

"I'm here," came the words, as outside early-evening light seeped into the room. Da stood in the open doorway, stripped to the waist. His shirt was balled around something in his hands.

Little Paddy jumped to his feet. "More berries?"

"Better." Da shut the door behind him, and the room went dim again. But we could see by the fluttering candlelight and the hearth fire and by the slight haze that filtered in through the smoke hole in our branch-and-peat roof. He put his bundle on the floor and opened it up. A spiny gray ball sat there.

Muc lifted her head from the corner where she'd been sleeping on her side. Her big piggy snout wiggled as she sucked in the new scent. Then she flopped her head back to the earthen floor and closed her eyes again.

Little Paddy went over to stand half behind Da. "What is it?"

"Wait and see."

But I knew. I'd seen them in the fields at dusk. Not the spud fields—the only animals I'd ever seen eat spud leaves were red deer. Not even our cow, Bo Bo, ate them. Those leaves were poisonous, after all. But in the grain fields in the evening, little fellows like that ball on the ground, just a lot larger, ran through all wobbly-like. They let out quick grunts that made me laugh.

After a few moments the hedgehog unrolled itself. It wandered off Da's shirt toward little Paddy's feet. The boy took a step back.

"Don't be afraid," I whispered. "He won't hurt."

"He's all pointy."

"But not mean. Besides, I'm pretty sure he's a baby. Don't you think he's cute?"

Little Paddy nodded. He stood very still as the hedgehog poked about his toes. Then he giggled. It must have tickled. Why was my brother so lucky with animals today? First the blue moth, now the hedgehog.

Muc had gotten up at the commotion. The pig walked over. She thrust her snout out to touch the hedgehog.

The hedgehog shrieked.

Muc squealed.

Now one was in a ball again, tighter than ever—and the other was back in the corner again, faster than ever.

We all laughed.

Da shook his head at Muc. "The big coward." He smiled and slapped himself on the chest. "For a moment there I thought I was going to have to whack her hard to keep her from eating our meal."

"Our meal?" asked little Paddy. "Berries? Muc eats all the old rot from last year. She doesn't need our berries." He knelt as the hedgehog unrolled again. "But maybe our new baby needs berries. Can I feed him one? From my cup, I mean. Can I?"

"You cannot," said Da. "This creature is—"

Ma put up a hand. "A silent mouth is sweet to hear." She gave Da a hard look.

And I got it. Little Paddy had no idea, but I understood like Ma did—I knew what Da had been about to say. My heart pounded in my ears. "The fields are green, Da. Think on that, please, Da, think on that. In just a few weeks, we can start digging up the fields. We won't be hungry anymore."

Da blinked at me. "Don't act thick. This isn't the usual hunger. It's not what we get toward the end of summer every year, when the last year's crop is all gone and the new year's isn't yet harvested and people beg along the roadside for two or three months. That's all normal. *Thruaill*—wretched—but normal. This isn't." Da shook his head. "Last year's harvest was ruined. People have been begging along the roadside ever since. Not just a couple of summer months, but all year long. Look at us—farmers. Farmers! And still, we've been hungry as the rest of them all year long."

"Right," I said quickly. I'd heard him spout those very words so many times, it felt polished, like a sermon in church. "Right, right. So what's a few more weeks, then?" I slid my eyes toward little Paddy and back to Da. "Think on it, Da! We'll have spuds this time next month. Lots. Harvest will be good, like it used to be, not like last year. We'll have spuds everywhere."

"The very best food in the world," said Ma in a lilting tone. "It's cruel how beautiful they are. And there will be enough to make your poteen again this year—something grand to drink in the evening. The treasure from all your spudding."

"Spuds," said Da softly. Then, "Spuds," even softer. His face gradually changed, till he wore that contented look he used to get after he'd been drinking poteen all evening—a look I hadn't seen for so long now.

"Exactly. That's what our mouths are watering for." Ma put

a hand on little Paddy's head. "No berries for the hedgehog, you hear, son? He's eaten enough of whatever he needs for today, I'm sure. And tomorrow you can follow him about outside, and he'll eat what he wants just out in the open. That's the best way with animals."

"We feed Muc."

"Muc's different. Look at Bo Bo, she just grazes all day. That's what most animals do, and it's especially true with wild things."

Da dropped onto his stool at the table with a loud sigh. "I could sure use a mug of poteen right now." He shut his eyes a second. There hadn't been enough spuds to make poteen last autumn, so Da had gone without all year. When he opened his eyes again, he didn't look at us.

We all took our places. We ate the gruel Ma had made from nettles and thickened with yellow cornmeal from America. The meal tasted good enough and sat heavy in the stomach, which was a relief. But, oh, I was sick of nettles. We'd had them all month it seemed . . . all summer, even. Still, they had a nice zingy taste and they didn't make us gassy like thistles did. Burdock was the best of the wild greens, though—tangy and crunchy. I reminded myself to go on a burdock hunt soon.

In any case, the buttermilk that followed the gruel was thick and just the right amount of sour to go with the sweet berries.

Little Paddy held the hedgehog in his lap with one hand while he ate. The animal was silent. I hoped it wasn't hurt. "What'll we call him?"

"No name," said Da.

Ma put her hand on Da's arm, but she kept her eyes on little Paddy. "Not yet, son. Like Da says. Wait till you know him better and can choose a name that fits."

When Da put his spoon down, he started his telling. Little Paddy and I settled onto our grass-and-straw mat on the floor. Almost instantly, my stomach rebelled. I had expected that, of course; that's what happened after eating nettles. Ma said they were hard to digest. I flopped around a long while, trying to get comfortable, then I got up and dragged our sleeping mat over near Muc. The night was growing frigid fast, and our pig was a grand source of heat as well as distraction from the pain in my belly. Besides, she smelled good. She was just like people—her waste stank, but her body gave off a lulling sweetness.

Muc wriggled around in her sleep till her snout was facing our mat. She had always preferred to sleep head-to-head with us. I didn't know why, but I liked it. It felt friendly. Her trotters moved as though she was running. I hoped her dream was fun.

Ma came with the old willow basket that Granny used to keep her unspun wool in. She took the no-name hedgehog from little Paddy and plopped it into the basket quick with a cloth over the top opening. She put her finger to her mouth to hush the boy, keep him from protesting in the middle of Da's telling. Then she tucked the basket into the crook of little Paddy's arm, and glanced quickly at Da and right back to us. We knew what that meant: Pay attention to the telling.

It was hard at first to ignore the hedgehog grunts that came from the basket. But Da's telling was grand tonight—and soon it filled my head. It was the story of the piper who knew only one tune and played that one badly. Terribly, in fact. But then he met a magic puca who gave him the gift of playing grand, like a master. The puca only had to name a tune and the piper found himself playing it marvelously.

I closed my eyes. I could imagine that stunned piper listening to the glory that came out of his own lungs. Oh, how I wished I could have the gift of music. The two best things in life were listening to music and listening to tellings. I loved to sing, but I had the voice of a sick frog.

Da's voice was rhythmic, like a drum; he was telling the best part now. The bewitched piper played for rich folk in a home as grand as the castle that the owner of our land lived in. But the food was served by the strangest fellow—a big white gander. And the piper recognized that gander as the same one he'd stolen from the priest, old Father William, on the Martinmas before. He'd eaten that very gander's wing.

Now that was a good trick—being eaten and coming back to life again. The best trick. I loved the whole idea. All you'd need was one goose, and you could eat him over and over. Even the poorest of the poor wouldn't go hungry. I hugged myself and smiled into the dark.

But no! What if the gander remembered being eaten? Teeth sinking into his flesh. I shivered.

Still, he wouldn't. That didn't make a good story—so he just wouldn't.

I listened more closely to Da.

After that meal, the piper played terribly again. The noise

he made was the screech of squabbling ganders. But then he went to old Father William and confessed all, and when the piper played next . . . oh, glory! His music was melodious beyond measure. He was the best piper of all the land.

I heard Da blow out the candle, then settle onto the big mat with Ma. She sang the wordless melody she sang every night. Soon Da was snoring—muffley-wuffley sounds that usually gave me comfort. Beside me little Paddy lay asleep as well—each breath a sweet sigh. And from the basket came the occasional scritch-scratch of that lovey little hedgehog.

But there was something wrong tonight. I listened close. There was an extra *plunk plunk* behind Da's snores. And then there were lots of *plunk*s between the snores too. It was raining. Harder and harder. Bucketing, in fact. In autumn or winter, I'd have thought nothing of it. But now? In August?

I chewed on the side of my thumb. My last thought was of a puca, smiling with a mouth that looked suspiciously like Ma's, and offering to pluck the frog from my throat.

CHAPTER THREE

Black

Da's shout woke me. He slopped through the mud, up and down the furrows between the hilled rows of plants, shouting, "No!" Just that one word. Over and over.

"Brutal," said Ma in a dead voice. She stood just outside our doorway, squinting into the low white fog.

I came to stand beside her.

"One night. The work of a single night." She shifted closer to me. "How could it happen? Last year wasn't this way. It wasn't. I remember everything. It's impossible to forget. The news from some island in England. Then from Belgium and France. Then, finally, here. But slow. Day by day. We watched everything wither day by day. Last year was awful . . . but this is worse. There's been no news from anywhere else. And there's nothing day by day about it. This is like a snap of some giant dragon's jaws." She shook her head slowly. "And it's the spuds again. The only crop we can't live without. Brutal."

The stalks of all those plants were still green—a taunting green, in fact, because the leaves dangled loosely, black as though scorched. Ruined. All in one night. Impossible. And Ma was right. The cabbages were still light green, the kale still dark green. Only the spuds had been ruined. The heart of every meal—or what used to be the heart.

Diabolical rain.

I hugged myself against the cold. Last year the plants had stayed green till almost harvesttime. We had listened to the news about other places and we thought we'd been spared. Then over the space of a month, our plants withered. And in October we dug up a mess—ruined spuds. Everything was different this time around; everything bad was happening earlier and faster.

"Grab a tool, Lorraine." Ma already held a spud digger, as though she'd woken prescient. "We must dig fast and save what we can."

I looked around. "What about Bo Bo?" The cow was usually standing at the door by this time of morning. If we ever overslept, her pained lowing woke us.

Ma looked around too. "The downpour last night must have confused her. Go find her and milk her. Then come dig. Fast."

I rushed inside and grabbed the milking bucket, then looked over at little Paddy. He stared at me, both hands around the hedgehog clutched to his chest. His eyes bore into me. *Pointy*, he mouthed silently. *We have to save Pointy.* So he had named the hedgehog even though Da had told him not to. And, worse, he knew what Da had intended last night, he knew after all. He'd just pretended not to—as though by pretending, he could make it not be true. I swallowed a lump of pain. Little Paddy was five. He shouldn't understand harsh things yet. I didn't think I did at his age.

I went and knelt beside my brother and turned the basket on its side. I whispered in his ear, "They'll think he escaped. Run out back and relieve yourself. No one will know."

"Ma will see."

"Not if Muc runs with you."

A tear welled in one eye, but he nodded.

I kicked Muc hard in the rump. The pig scrambled to her feet. She gave me a hurt look with her deep-set, squinty eyes and pressed her snout against my belly. But there was no way to explain to her. I rubbed her ears the way she liked, in the hopes that she'd remember that later and forgive me. Then I did the only thing I could think of: I kicked her again. Harder. She ran out the door with little Paddy behind her, him bent over as though his belly ached, hiding that sweet ball of love. Ma didn't give either of them a second glance.

I clumped out after them and walked randomly here and there, looking for Bo Bo. I didn't have to search long. As soon as that cow heard me singing, she came lumbering from a low hill and bashed me in the chest with her wide forehead. I wondered if she had learned that behavior from Muc, or if Muc had learned it from her, or if it was just natural to all pigs and cows. Bo Bo pushed insistently. A cow that needs milking isn't shy. At this rate, she'd knock me over. I rubbed her under the neck so she'd lift her chin. Then I set to work.

I squirted myself a hot, sweet mouthful and wished we had four cows, and I sang as I milked her right there in the grass, just to save time. After all, she walked far slower than me—so this way I could get the milk home faster. When her udder was empty and slack again, Bo Bo went down on her front knees, one then the other. She folded her rear legs, then, *plop*, she dropped to the ground with a groan. She looked so shattered, I wondered if she'd been awake all night, frightened by the deluge. Had she climbed that hill to get away from a flood? Did she catch a glimpse of the distant mountains of Connemara all purple in the night and wish she could climb to the top of them? Did she know that much? I doubted it; I couldn't remember her ever doing anything that seemed cunning. I scratched her under the neck again. Bo Bo never showed the slightest sign of affection, not like Muc, but at least it was clear she enjoyed being scratched. And she didn't give out at my singing—never a complaint; I liked her for that. A lot. I walked back to our cottage, careful not to spill a drop. After all, we shared with the cottier families these days, which meant there would be barely enough.

The cottage was empty; everyone else was working already. I put the milk inside and grabbed a spud digger.

We dug spuds all morning, the four of us, under a sun that turned hot and hotter. Every overturned lump of mud polluted the air worse. The stench turned my stomach. Most of the spuds were small, the size Da called haws, and some were even smaller, the size of thimbles—far from ready to be taken from the ground. In the old days we would have saved spuds this size as seed for the planting the next spring. But Da and Ma were right to dig now because many spuds were black already. They must have been turning black under the dirt for days before— and we hadn't even guessed. The rot had started from below, as though it had been lurking there since last year.

Still, many others were green and brown. I couldn't check their smell because my nose was so full of the smell of the putrid black ones. But their color mattered; green and brown—that had to be good.

Toward midday a man came riding up on a horse. He worked for the landlord, but I didn't know his name. Da glanced at him, then kept digging spuds, in ground that had gone from sloppy to almost rocky under the baking sun. The man rode all the way up to Da, stopped, and dismounted.

"You're supposed to be in the grain fields with your cottiers. This is harvesting season for grain, not potatoes."

Though he said it in English, not Irish, I understood perfectly. We lived on English land—and Da insisted that we practice English among ourselves so that when the landlord or his men barked at us, we could answer all polite-like in their language. It was easy to practice. Da had grown up speaking only Irish, but Ma grew up speaking English more than Irish and she was a good model for us all. Little Paddy and I spoke it well, far better than Da. Two of the cottier mas and one of the das grew up with English too, so all the kids on this farm spoke it at least a little.

Da straightened to full height. He was taller than this Englishman. Ma liked to say all Irish grew taller than English, but even I knew that wasn't true. Da looked down his nose at the man. "Spuds that stay in this earth will turn rotten, unfit to feed a family. Unfit even as food for swine."

"These potatoes are lumpers—I can't understand why all of you grow the same variety. Lumper potatoes don't even taste good. You don't need them. Eat your turnips and cabbage."

"And just how long do those sustain a body?" said Da. "A lumper fills the belly."

"Bah! You grow wheat and oats, too. Eat them."

Da shook his head. "If we're forced to eat the grains we grow, we'll have nothing to sell to pay the rent."

"You're in the middle of the grain harvest. The very middle. The morning sun has dried them well now. Who knows if the rain is going to start up again any minute. Best to make use of the sun. If you lose this grain harvest . . ."

Da dropped his spud digger and stomped back and forth up the furrow. Then he stopped and nodded at the man. The man rode off.

Da looked at us. "The steward's right. You have to finish without me. I'm fetching the cottiers. Go talk to their wives. See if you can get them to help you."

Ma didn't even answer. She had never stopped digging. Little Paddy and I went back to work. I listened to him chanting under his breath, "Dig dig dig."

We rested in late afternoon and Ma roasted us a big spud each, right in the hearth ashes. The three biggest ones we'd dug up so far. There were brownish and purplish spots under the skin of mine, but inside most of it was white—and all of it tasted good. Better than good; it was the best food ever. We gobbled them fast, me fastest of all, and I thought at first my stomach might rebel and spill it all out again. But it behaved. We hadn't had spuds since December, when we ran out of those we'd salvaged from the wasted harvest last autumn. Ma had managed to make them last that long only by rationing them severely. The murrain—the deadly illness—had stolen more than half our harvest. Lots more. This year wasn't so bad. No, I was sure it wasn't. It couldn't be. We were digging them up fast. The cull pile—unfit for anyone but Muc—was huge, but the pile of good ones was already as tall as little Paddy. They were smaller, they were, but there were lots of them.

"We have plenty more spuds this time around, Ma," I said. When she didn't look at me, I added, "They'll last longer this time . . . longer than last year . . . well into winter . . . maybe all the way till spring. You're good at making them last."

She looked at me now, and her face was so shattered, I flinched. It was as though she'd become an old lady in just the space of a day. She nodded. "Finish up. You'll never plow a field by turning it over in your mind." She licked her fingers, and I knew they were burnt from handling the roasted spuds when they were so hot. She grabbed her tool and went back to digging.

Little Paddy whispered in my ear, "You think she's gone in the head? Like Granny was?"

"What?"

"You know. Maybe she got it passed down from Granny."

"Granny was Da's ma, not Ma's."

"I don't know how, but somehow she's gone in the head."

"Why do you say that, Paddy?"

"We're not plowing. She said we had to go plow."

"It's just a way of talking," I whispered back. "Memorize it. Use it when you need to."

"Why doesn't she call the cottier wives, like Da said? They'd get this all done a lot faster."

"And if they came to help us, just who do you think would be digging up the spuds in their own gardens? Who'd save their families?"

"Huh?"

"Get to work." I pinched his arm.

Sometimes little Paddy seemed to know things—like this morning with the hedgehog. Other times he seemed to know nothing. The digging had to be done now—no time to lose. Whatever didn't get pulled out of the ground today would be that much more rotted by tomorrow. And the day after that, the ground might hold only mush. That's what happened last year. . . . When it was finally clear the crop was really failing, we'd had to work fast. Plus, the ground was already baked hard now. If the sun stayed, the ground would grow harder each day, and it would be that much more work to dig spuds.

Against my will, I thought of the cottier wives with their strong arms and hands and how much faster this would all go if they were digging with us now. Four cottier families lived on the land we rented. Da was a tenant farmer, and a poor one at that. Some of the other tenant farmers had homes with three rooms. Our cottage was just one room. Da said we shouldn't be envious, though, because those farmers kept manure in their houses just like we did, and they, in fact, owned nothing, just like us.

Despite what he said, I was envious. Not of the other tenant farmers; no, not them. Of the landlords. Everyone knew this land used to belong to us Irish. But now the English owned it. When I'd asked Ma and Da how that had happened, Da had started to talk, but Ma stopped him. She said it was behind us, and that meant it didn't matter.

So this was how it was: They owned the big houses. And the castles.

And they owned the land, while we were just tenant farmers.

Still, all tenant farmers rented the land legally, so we had rights.

The cottiers were far worse off. They were workers without any lawful home. They helped Da in all the chores in the fields: plowing, seeding, and mostly harvesting—the oats and wheat and everything. In return Da helped them build huts in a little cluster on the stoniest part of the ten acres we farmed. And near their huts they had their own private kitchen gardens, just like we did, to feed their families—one garden per hut. Full of spuds. There were eighteen children altogether in the four families. Ma used to say, her voice all wistful, that the cottier wives were lucky to have so many little ones. She hadn't said that for a long time now, though.

They were hungry, those cottier families. But they were strong—like us. Their mas were just as resourceful as our ma at making broth from kale and cabbage and weeds, and just as severe at doling out the spuds.

The only one who died on this land last year because of the lack of spuds was Granny.

It wasn't because she was gone in the head, like little Paddy thought. And it wasn't because she was weak. It was because she simply stopped eating, so she could give her share of greens or turnips to the rest of us. That was something little Paddy didn't know, something that made my chest squeeze so tight it hurt. I hoped little Paddy grew old without figuring it out. Ma and Da would never say it. But I knew it was true. Granny had done something awful.

Sometimes even the best of us did something awful.

I pressed the back of my forearm against my eyelids. Just for a moment.

Little Paddy was working hard now. So was I. We dug spuds all the rest of the day. When Da got home, he joined us. We dug spuds all through the evening. Then I milked Bo Bo again, and by the time I came inside, we were ready to feast. This time Ma had boiled the spuds and we ate them with the skins. The mealy parts were hardly noticeable. Three apiece for little Paddy and me, four for Ma, and a pile for Da. Seven, actually. I tried hard not to count them, but I couldn't help it. Somehow, the more spuds I ate, the more spuds I wanted. But Da was bigger than us, he needed more. And I was glad he was big. His size alone made us all feel safe. He could work longer hours than anyone.

We went to bed without a telling. I was too shattered to care, though. Too full of aches. I sprawled on the mat, itchy all over just from being so plain dirty. But even that couldn't keep me awake. My eyes closed before Ma's lullaby ended.

The next day was the same, only harder because the dirt was in clumps solid as clay and our bodies were already bruised from the first day of digging. But Ma made little Paddy and me sing with her as we worked, and that helped. Singing was magic. By nighttime we'd finished the entire plot.

So the third day we shifted to the next job—loading those spuds into the pit. We had to layer them with ferns. It hadn't rained again, not since the night it lashed so hard. That was good, at least for this part of the job; the ferns were dry, the spuds were dry. No new moisture to encourage rot.

We wiped the spuds as free of dirt as we could and were ready to throw them in the pit, when Ma lay a staying hand on my shoulder. "Do you think we should put the ones that look the best on the bottom, because they'll last longer—and put the ones that are already going bad on top, so we can eat them sooner?"

That sounded right. I nodded.

"But what if the worst ones on top make the best on the bottom rot faster? Do you think instead we should put the worst on the bottom and the best on top? That way we'll at least get the best ones before they rot."

I had no idea what we should do. I didn't move. I didn't want Ma to read any flicker of my eye or twitch of my lips as an answer. I held my breath.

"Or maybe we should sell the best now, and save the worst for eating. No one would buy the worst ones—but they'd buy the best ones, don't you think? That way we'll at least have money later when our spuds run out, and we can buy from others." Her brow wrinkled and she shook her head. "But I'm thinking all wrong—no one else will have spuds to sell then."

"We can buy grains," said little Paddy.

Ma looked at him as though in shock. "Don't act thick, Paddy. Spuds bring only four shillings per hundredweight—oats bring seventeen shillings. We could never buy oats—at least, not nearly enough oats to make up for selling our best spuds."

What a thought. We grew those oats, but we were too poor to buy the product of our own labor. That felt so wrong it made my head spin.

"So, then," said Ma, "we put them all in the pit." She stared at me now. Waiting. It was up to me!

My heart raced. "Let's make a second pit," I said at last. "Then we'll have one for the best spuds and one for the worst."

Ma came over and kissed me on the forehead. "Cunning girl. Like your da always says."

So that's what we did.

CHAPTER FOUR

Recipes

How big was yours?"

Emmet stared at Quinlin. "Bigger than my hand." He held one hand out as though it was holding a huge boiled spud, and with his other hand he mimicked peeling the jacket off it in just one swift slice of his thumbnail.

I could hardly imagine a spud that big . . . not now in October. Any big spuds there were had been eaten long ago.

Quinlin blinked. "Flat like that, or curled in a fist?"

"Flat."

"I don't believe you."

Emmet stood up and swaggered toward Quinlin.

"None of that carrying on," said Deirdre. "Sit down, Emmet." Deirdre was thirteen, only a year older than me, but she had the weight of authority in her voice. Plus she held baby Nola in her arms, which made her seem that much more in charge. Baby Nola's hair stuck out in every direction all fuzzy and soft. I wanted to pet it.

When little Paddy was just a babe, I used to carry him around everywhere like that. I pulled little Paddy onto my lap now, big as he was.

"I don't have to listen to you." Emmet frowned at Deirdre.

"You're big sister to Nola and Quinlin, but you're nothing to me."

"But I'm big sister to you, I am," said Alana. "Sit down. No one cares how big your spud was, anyway."

"I care," said Riley.

So did I. I wished I'd had a spud that big at the midday meal this Sunday. Oh, I knew Emmet had to be exaggerating. As Ma said, *for some people all their geese were swans.* But I still bet Emmet's was big. We had only small ones left, and few at that. After the initial digging back in August, with that amazing splurge of spuds, we'd had only one each at the midday meal and one each at the evening meal—Ma and little Paddy and me. Da got two, of course. No one could argue with that. It was pitiful little for a grown man. Pitiful little for all of us.

But even so, Ma's careful rationing wasn't going to help for long. Only two months had passed since the murrain hit and that much was already clear.

I was there beside him each time Da went to the spud pits. I helped him lift off the turf he had covered the pits with as protection against thieves, human and animal, and I helped push aside the ferns underneath. I stood there speechless with him as we stared at the mess. Spuds that had looked healthy when they were pulled from the dirt were rotting fast in storage.

And in both pits. So I wasn't cunning after all.

Last week Da and all the other tenant farmers on the estate had gathered on the lawn outside the landlord's castle and begged for help. There was nothing to eat. *Food, for pity's sake, food.* Little Paddy and I peeked from behind the old stone wall and saw it all and heard it all. The men said things I'd never known before—awful things about what people had done because they were desperate. A few times I put my hands over little Paddy's ears, but he scratched them off.

The landlord said he knew the crop had been unfavorable. *Unfavorable? It had failed,* they said. He grimaced, but said there would be no handouts on his property—that was surely the way to ruin trade. Handouts? They were starving, they said. I hated that word: *starving.* Others said it a lot, but we never even whispered it in our home—as though saying it would bring it on. The landlord insisted that rotten spuds mixed with seaweed were a nutritious meal—even some fancy duke somewhere had said that. That was no answer at all; we all knew how sick we got from eating rot. The landlord would never understand that. So the tenant farmers begged for jobs through the winter. How was a farmer to survive otherwise? But the landlord asked, what jobs? He had no use for tenant farmers during the cold months. And that was the end of that.

Just last night I'd heard Da tell Ma that the pits would be empty soon. Ma had planted extra cabbage and kale right after the murrain, and they were coming in now, big enough to eat. The yield from this planting would last till spring. But Ma said cabbage and kale didn't put flesh on bones. And they sure didn't satisfy like spuds.

This was trouble. Worse trouble than we'd ever known.

I looked around at the expectant faces of my friends. "Who's telling?"

"Telling? I'm for hurling," said Emmet. He was still

standing—and all I could think was, *Poor Alana.* She was the oldest among us and she was always fair and wise. But she had a horrible, disobedient little brother. Emmet turned in a circle to look at all of us. "Our Sundays were a lot more fun together when we played. Who votes for hurling?"

"No one else had a spud as big as yours at the midday meal today," said Riley. "No one else has the energy to run after the ball."

"Aw, cop on! How can you be so thick? Your da's grand at hurling. You'll be grand at hurling if you just stop being a puss face and give it a try."

Alana got up and pushed on Emmet's shoulders, till he was sitting like the rest of us. "I've got a good story."

"So what?" said Emmet. "I've heard all your stories. Besides, good stories don't fill the belly."

"Neither does hurling," said Carrick.

"Do any of you know what haggis is?" said Fiona.

"I do," said little Aeden.

"Me too," said Corey.

Fiona put her hand up to hush them. "Don't be thick. Naturally, you do, Aeden and Corey. We . . ." She looked across Murray and Neil and Iona. "We all do in our family. I'm asking the others, the ones who aren't our brothers or sisters."

"You win, Fiona," said Carrick. "What's haggis?"

"It's Scottish." Fiona nodded at us all. "Our ma used to make it. She grew up way over in Scotland. Close your eyes and I'll tell you how it's made."

"What's the point of that?" said Carrick.

"Just shut your gob and listen. First, you take a sheep stomach."

"Sheep stomach stinks," said Carrick.

"What do you know?" said Corey. He squeezed his eyes shut tight.

"All animal stomachs stink," said Carrick.

"Just hush!" Fiona clapped sharp and fast. "I'll belt the next person who speaks. I'm doing the talking now. Just me. So . . . you take a sheep stomach and you wash the inside out really good. Good good good. Then you rub salt into it and you wash it again. By that point, it doesn't stink; it doesn't smell at all." Fiona nodded at us. "Sometimes there's fat globs hanging on and sometimes stringy things. You rip those off and you soak the whole thing in cold salty water for hours. Then you turn the stomach inside out."

Emmet cleared his throat and opened his mouth.

"No one speaks but me!" Fiona pointed at Emmet. "No one! Don't be bold." She made a mean face at all of us. "Now, while the stomach is soaking . . . before you turn it inside out . . . you boil the sheep heart and liver—then you chop them up."

Kearney groaned as though in disgust.

Alana punched Kearney in the shoulder and rolled her eyes heavenward. I felt sorry for her, being the big sister of both Emmet and Kearney. It was too much for any girl to bear. I kissed little Paddy on the top of the head.

"Now you take oatmeal and toast it brown. Then mix it with the liver and heart and add nice things—like salt and pepper and nutmeg." Fiona took a deep breath, as though she was smelling those ingredients. "And you put in some fat from the kidneys. That's important." She folded her hands together under her chin. "So important." She licked her bottom lip. "Then tuck it all into the stomach. You have to leave plenty of room for the oats to swell up. And you sew it tight, then drop it in a pot of stock—you know, the water left from boiling the heart and liver—and cook it for hours."

Fiona stopped speaking.

We all waited, eyes on Fiona. Even Corey looked at her now.

"Are you done?" asked Carrick.

"I am. Wasn't that delicious?"

"It was blather," said Kearney. "Garbage."

"And a fib," said Emmet.

"A fib?" Fiona thrust her chin toward Emmet. "I never tell fibs."

"You did this time," said Emmet. "If you boil a sewed-up stomach, it'll explode."

Lots of kids laughed and whispered.

"You're all thick," said Murray. "You make little holes in it before you boil it. Just knife pricks. Anyone knows that. My sister doesn't fib. Take it back, Emmet. Take it back right now!"

"I take it back," said Emmet. "You don't need to bite my head off. I take it back for sure. But haggis is still garbage."

"No it's not," said Corey. "And when Fiona was telling, I shut my eyes and you know what? I tasted that haggis. I loved it. And now I feel full."

"Full?" said Emmet.

"Nearly," said Corey.

"I feel satisfied too," said Teagan. "I love anything with haslet—that's what my first ma used to call those things, liver and heart and lungs and stuff. It was a wonderful telling, Fiona."

"I agree," said Sheelagh.

"Me too," said Noreen.

"Good, then I'll tell a recipe with spuds," said Kyla. "Something my whole family loves—including Emmet and Kearney. And we'll all feel full. So . . . you chop boiled cabbage."

"Stop," said Neil. "Don't tell it like that. All fast and businesslike. Tell it slow. Like Fiona did."

"Yeah," said Quinlin. "Make it a real telling. Every detail. Right from the start with picking the cabbage. Fiona did it that way—just like our da. That's how to do it."

So their da did tellings too. And suddenly I wondered, did they get together every night—all four cottier families—for one big telling? We were the tenant farmers, but we were isolated. They were just cottier families, but they had one another. When Ma used to call the cottier wives lucky, I thought she was wrong; we were the lucky ones in so many ways. But now I was sensing something new. I wriggled over closer to Alana, pulling little Paddy along.

"I understand," said Kyla. "I'll tell every detail. Let's see. You start in the garden. It's late afternoon and it's been a normal day—cool and drizzly. Can you feel it on your skin? You're all gooseflesh, you know. Feel it?"

"I don't feel it," said Emmet. "I want to hear about the food. Try to fill us up."

"Shut your eyes," piped up little Paddy.

"Huh?" said Emmet.

"He's right," I said. "If we shut our eyes, we'll listen better. Like Corey did—he said with his eyes shut he tasted the haggis. If we shut our eyes, we'll be able to feel what Kyla's saying."

"I'm waiting," said Kyla. She looked around at all of us. "Shut your eyes."

I shut mine.

"You walk slow among the cabbages. Ah, there's a nice big one. You squeeze it. It's firm through and through. You cut it off right—so that you leave behind a nice fat stem. That way you'll get lots of sprouts on the stem later." She gave a loud sigh. "I love the little sprouts later. You wash that head, but you don't have to wash it like Fiona's sheep stomach because it's not disgusting."

Lots of laughter.

"The tight leaves keep the inside clean," Kyla went on. "So boil it. Then just chop it up. Slice one direction, then slice the other. And that nice smell will fill the room."

"I can smell it," said someone. I was pretty sure it was Murray. "Like a fart from a pished old man."

More laughter.

"Shut up. I love cabbage," said someone else. "And you better too, since soon it'll be the best we get till next autumn." I was almost entirely sure that was Emmet talking.

"Spuds," said Kyla. "Bring your minds back to spuds. Now you take those spuds from the pit. Oh, there's no job in choosing them. The pit is full of hard spuds—all of them healthy. They aren't small like now, but big, really big, full-grown spuds, all of them. And all of them smell of nothing but dirt. Just holding them makes you smile. Feel how solid they are in your hand? You can toss them in the air and they come back down into your hand with a hard slap. Nothing mushy."

"Perfect spuds," said someone.

"I feel them," said someone else. "I've got one in each hand. And they smell just like dirt."

"You don't have to take just two. You can take as many as you want. Enough to be equal to the cabbage. The pit is full—"

"Full? When's . . ."

"This is my telling, I'm in charge, and I say the pit is full. But you wash those spuds good—not like the cabbage—because dirt is bad to eat. You put them in water, and you rub and rub. Then you boil them."

"You really boil them with the cabbage," said someone close by.

"Right, Alana. I should have said that. Anyway, after you chop the cabbage, you chop the spuds. You slice and slice."

"I smell them," said someone. "Those spuds. All fresh."

"I feel the heat rising from them as they split," said someone else.

"They're so hot, they scald. But you're cunning. You know if you took a bite now, you'd be licking the burn on the roof of your mouth for days. So you don't do that. You eat their smell, but you don't eat them. Not yet. Ah, spuds. These ones are soft from boiling, so they fall apart fast. In a big bowl you mix them—the spuds and the cabbage. You add lots of salt. Lots. And then pepper."

"Not too much," said someone. I think it was Kearney.

"Right, Kearney, my love. Just enough. And you put in butter. Plenty of butter. Enough to make it all smooth and lovely."

"Shiny yellow butter," said someone.

The kind we make from Bo Bo's milk. Pure yellow.

"And a bit of vinegar. Not a splash. Just a drop. Then it's perfect. Put it in a stew pan over the fire. And stir and stir, so it doesn't stick. You serve it hot. And you eat it. You're eating it now. It's hot in your mouth—not burning anymore, just hot. And it's soft and fluffy with just enough solid bits. You push it all around your mouth with your tongue. It slides down into your stomach. Bite after bite after bite."

Kyla went quiet.

"It's the best," said Kearney. "Once on Christmas, Ma served it with cold salted meat. I like it plain, though. It's the best."

I opened my eyes and looked around almost dazed. My mouth could taste that buttery dish. My stomach was happy.

"I'm full," said Emmet.

I was too.

"So that's it," said Quinlin. "Every Sunday our tellings will be recipes."

I couldn't wait till next Sunday.

Part 2

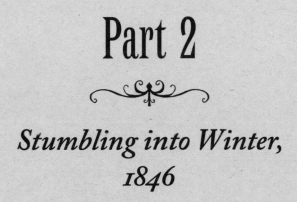

Stumbling into Winter,
1846

CHAPTER FIVE

Foraging

Lorraine, remember those blackberries?"

Those lusciously juicy berries of summer. I closed my eyes for just a second and my mouth could taste them, even months later. "Of course I do, Ma."

"You said lavender and peppermint grew near the brambles along the sides of a stream."

"They did. Lots of them."

"They were in the woods, were they?"

"They were, Ma."

"You're a cunning girl. Go back there and find wood sorrel for me, would you? Just be wide. You can do that; you know how to take care of yourself."

"It's the start of December, Ma." Cold, too. That damp cold that made my teeth ache. I pressed my fingers on my lips at the thought.

"You might still find some. And if you don't, gather whatever other plants you can. We have to add something special to the gruel, something inviting. We have to get Paddy eating hearty again. I want him strong before Christmas."

None of us was eating hearty. But I couldn't say that to Ma, not with her face as lined as it was now. She'd done all she could. Despite her severe rationing, the spuds had run out weeks ago. And though the government cornmeal cost only a penny a pound, we'd run out of money, too. No more yellow meal. The thin gruel since then just ran through us like water. I was already sick of kale. I looked at the bare shelf behind Ma and thought of what tonight's meal would be like, us sitting on stools around the table—our only furniture—and biting our tongues. Talking about what you can't fix just makes it hurt more. "Something's bound to be growing. I'll go fetch Paddy." He was lying on our mat in the corner, still asleep.

"Don't do that. Leave your brother here. I don't want him wasting his strength trying to walk uphill. He'll stay with me."

"Kiss him for me, Ma." I went out the door.

"Wait. Take the gathering basket." She came out after me and put it over my wrist. "How much sorrel could you carry in your bare hands, after all?"

I took the basket and nodded.

"Let's hold on to hope, Lorraine. Make it a beautiful day, my beautiful daughter."

"Every day is beautiful, Ma. Look how green it is." And even though I knew I was simply echoing what Granny used to say, I realized it was true. The withered, black ruins of the diseased potato plants had long ago turned to nothing, and everywhere you looked was green. Brilliant shades of green. I loved how the land was green year-round. Not all places were like that, I knew. "Granny would have smiled out over what we're seeing now."

"She would have, Lorraine. But there's something Granny didn't understand. Listen to me. Listen close. Please understand." Ma stepped right up to me and tilted her head kindly. "You can't eat the view," she whispered.

I nodded. I didn't agree, though. Granny did understand that you couldn't eat the view. She absolutely understood. She had made a choice. But I clutched the basket handle tight and turned to go.

"Hello, there, young miss."

I gawked. A motley group had come up from behind our cottage. A man as thin as a sapling led it. Three naked children with bluish skin and snot crusted on their faces followed. They shivered in the icy air.

Ma had already gone back inside.

"Ma," I called.

She opened the door, and her face fell slack at the sight of the group. I was sure she was thinking the same that I was thinking: no woman.

"Sit down and I'll bring you each a bowl of gruel," she said.

"No spuds?" asked the man.

A sad laugh burst from Ma. "We haven't seen spuds for nearly a month now."

The man nodded. One heavy nod. "I can't remember when me and my snappers last saw them."

Little Paddy and Muc came out the door. Ma stepped toward them quick and pushed them back across the threshold to the inside.

"Just sit," said Ma to the group of strangers.

"You can see the snappers are cold," said the man. "Freezing. Can't we come in and sit by that hot pig?"

Ma shook her head.

"Ma!" I said.

She gave me a sharp look. Then she looked back at the man. "You know I can't allow that," she said in a gentle voice.

"We haven't been indoors in so long. The workhouse won't take us."

"I'm sorry to hear that. I'm very sorry. I'm a good Catholic woman. But I have to protect my family first."

"We're honest folk. We didn't come sneaking at night and rip up your turnips. We're here in daytime. We're honest. We wouldn't harm you."

"You wouldn't choose to, no. Never for a minute did I think that. But there used to be more than the four of you, now, didn't there?"

"Seven," said the man.

"See? And I bet they didn't go off to Canada in a ship, now, did they? Please, sit. I'll heat up the gruel and bring it out. It'll make a grand midday meal, if a bit early."

"Thank you."

"You're very welcome to it." She waved at me. "Get going, Lorraine. And find something. I don't care if you stay out late. What you gather can be for the evening meal. That will be fine. Just make us all smile when you come back."

I didn't like leaving Ma and little Paddy alone with that man and his waifs. I didn't understand why, but I wasn't so thick that I didn't realize her words to the da meant she was afraid of them in some unspoken way. Still, she had gone back inside and they were now sitting docilely on the cold dirt, their red-rimmed eyes staring at nothing. They didn't even huddle together for warmth; they had no warmth to share. They posed no danger I could help fight against, so there was nothing for me to do here.

And there was something important to do in the woods. I marched off, determined to come back with that basket full somehow. A handful of this, a handful of that. I could do it. The air bit at the bare skin on my arms, but I ignored it. I was strong, lots stronger than the man and his waifs. I wouldn't turn blue for hours.

I walked and walked, straight to the highest hill, on the other side of which was the peat bog. Starting at the foot of the hill, I wandered wide, right to left and back again, as I went up. I missed little Paddy. It would have been fun to have him along, noticing everything, birds and plants, and talking about them all, just being little Paddy. I imagined him picking the rare sweet flower here and there—daisies or chickweeds—and sticking one each behind his ears, and, when there was no room for more, behind mine. He was a funny boy. We were usually together all day long. I bet he missed me, too. But he had Ma. And probably Muc. That pig stayed inside more and more as the weather got colder.

I finally found the stream, much reduced now and hardly warmer than ice. The bare brambles on the bank were broken and ugly. The mint bent over, dry and yellow gray. The lavender stood in brown spikes.

But who cared? Because along the edge I spied the shiny, dark green leaves of watercress. I ran there and squatted in the middle of it and ripped up handfuls, along with their long, irregular roots. I loved the peppery taste. And beside this huge patch of cress, wild celery poked up tall stalks. Who cared, who cared, if the leaves were gone and the flowers were all dried up? The stalks were what mattered. I couldn't believe my luck.

The basket was already half full.

Still, Ma wanted wood sorrel. I thought about little Paddy chewing on a fleshy stem, smiling at the tartness. Ma was right, we needed sorrel. I scanned the banks of the stream. All different leaves, but none were heart-shaped with a fold down the middle. I went higher and higher up the hill. Nothing.

When I got to the top, I looked out over the land below. I saw the ruins of an ancient rock fort way over there, but no people anywhere, not a one—just a few slumped sheep in the distance and a small fluttering of collared doves overhead. Then I looked southward, to the Aran Islands, all gray and stark. And more south, to where the Cliffs of Moher stood. Would I ever see them?

The day was cold, perishing cold, and my breath puffed in tiny clouds under my nose. I put down the basket and rubbed my arms as hard as I could and tried to think of hot things to warm me up, but all I could think about was those three naked children. I was better off than them, I knew that. All of us slept on the ground—them and us alike. But my family had mats under us and a roof over our heads. That man and his waifs had nothing.

Still, I didn't feel as lucky as I knew Ma would tell me I was. My dress was worn thin and ripped in spots. I should have put on my jumper, even though it had gotten snug on me since last winter. Ma said she didn't know how I grew with so little food. Little Paddy hadn't grown at all, but I was at least a hand taller. She said I must eat the air itself. And she promised to make me a new one, as good as what Granny would have made. That was an amazing promise, because Granny made the best fishermen's jumpers ever. She'd made the one Da wore all the time, and it was grand. But where would we find the money to pay for a skein of wool? So I'd been putting off wearing that jumper; I didn't want to seem like I was pointing a finger at Ma. Giving out like some baby. I was no complainer. A shiver went up my spine.

I was suddenly glad little Paddy was home, by the peat fire and with Muc at his side. Warm and cozy in that smoke that smelled of fairies and mysteries. I could believe any telling, no matter how fantastic, if it happened by a peat-fed fire with Muc making grunty breaths beside me.

And, oh, I hoped the man and his waifs had left already. I didn't want them near little Paddy. Nor near Ma. I hoped they'd eaten their fill and were off somewhere else to beg.

Their fill. The idea almost brought a laugh. No one got full on kale gruel.

I looked down into the basket that still lacked sorrel. It was only midday, and the other side of this hill might hold entirely different plants. There was a chance, at least. So I trudged on. Down the far side. Down, down. But instead of heading toward the peat bog that Da and I visited a couple of times a week now, I went the other way. Beyond a small stand of bare trees and tall brown grasses, I saw the green meadow sloping up to the castle where our landlord lived. I wouldn't go all the way there, naturally. No one went to the castle without being summoned. And children never went. But that stand of trees on the way might hold dried berries or nuts.

As I got closer, I heard something. Talk. A lot of talk. Blather, really. Was that English? I crept forward as quiet as I could, moving from behind one trunk to behind the next.

And there, on the cold ground, sat a fancy girl. Not right on the ground, of course. She sat on a mat cover. Decked out in a green dress like none I'd ever seen before—long sleeves and a sash at the waist. A wool shawl went across her back and arms. A floral bonnet was tied on by a bow under her chin. Her legs were crossed in front of her, and I was behind her and off to the side a bit, so I couldn't see them. But I could see a black leather shoe sticking out on one side, under her bent knee. A grand shoe, hardly worn at all.

In the middle of the mat cover, a small and lacy square cloth was spread flat. The girl sat at one end of it. On the other three sides sat small miniatures of people. Dollies!

I had a dolly. Margaret. She was made from a goat shin. Da had carved out eyes and a mouth and used a natural bump near one end of the bone for the nose. The bump was off to one side, so it made Margaret's face imbalanced, and that meant her eyes were kind of funny, sort of on a slant. But I liked that. Those eyes made her more like real people. Granny had knitted her a dress and stuffed straw inside it, so that she looked like she had flesh surrounding the bone—but that dress came apart long ago. Good old Margaret. I couldn't remember where I'd put her. I hadn't played with her in the longest time.

The dollies here, though, they were totally different. With painted faces and hair that looked real and dresses as fancy as the girl's. I'd never seen anything so grand.

But my eyes passed over those dolls in a flash. They settled on what was in the middle of the white cloth: a feast. I gasped.

CHAPTER SIX

Feast

At my gasp the girl jumped to her feet. "Who are you?" She spoke in English.

I swallowed and forced my eyes from the feast to the girl. "Was that you talking before? Who were you talking to?"

"I asked first."

"I'm Lorraine."

"It's not nice to sneak up on people."

"I thought there were a lot of you."

"That doesn't make it nice. You're old enough to know better."

"You're right," I said. I hated it when people snuck up on me. "I'm sorry."

"Really?"

"Really."

"Well, then." She rocked her head side to side so hard, her whole body moved. It made me think of the old church bell. Her hair was brown like mine. But hers hung in curling loops down the sides of her face.

"So," I said, "who were you talking to?"

"My dolls."

"Oh."

"There's nothing wrong with talking to dolls."

I blinked.

"In case you were thinking it wasn't quite right, I mean. Plenty of girls older than me do it." She seemed to be waiting for an answer.

"Oh," I said.

"And there's no one else to talk to."

"I can see that," I said.

"Except you're here now. So we can have a real conversation. I love real conversations." The girl sat back in her spot and arranged her skirt across her knees. She looked up at me primly, expectation on her face. "Talk."

I didn't want to talk. Saliva had filled my mouth. The sight of that feast dazzled me.

"Sit down."

I sat.

"Not over there on the ground! Are you daft? You're Irish, aren't you? All Irish are daft. That's what Dad says. Come here and sit on the cover."

"I'm not daft."

"Dad knows these things."

"I'm not daft."

"Well . . . that remains to be seen. Sit."

Her da said Irish were daft. My da said English were bullies. Her da was wrong. But I was getting the feeling my da was right. Still, what was the harm in obeying her?

I walked around and sat on the very edge of the cover, on a corner as far from her as I could get. The smell of the feast made me swoon. "What is that?"

"What?"

I pointed.

"Roasted hare. Haven't you ever had roasted hare?"

I shook my head.

"That's absurd. Is your dad too lazy to hunt?"

I stiffened. None of us was a dosser; we all worked hard—even little Paddy. "Hunting rights belong to the landlord."

The girl frowned. "Well, I don't know what you mean by that. But the taste is lovely. Try some."

Could I have heard right? "What?"

"You can have Alexandra's share. But she doesn't have a fork or knife, so you have to eat with your fingers."

I looked around. What person in her right mind would give me her share? "Who's Alexandra?"

"The dolly beside you. Don't you love her red smock and apron? She has an umbrella, too, but we didn't bring it today because it's not raining, for once. And this"—she nodded her head toward another dolly—"is Eleanor. Look at her collar and cuffs. Have you ever seen such fine lace? Well, I wouldn't guess you had. It's handmade in Bedfordshire. Nearly as good as the queen's. And she"—she nodded her head toward the third dolly—"is Geraldine. I wanted at least one blond dolly, after all. Don't you think her green dress brings out her coloring?"

I would have paid better attention to this girl's blather under other circumstances—because, in fact, the dollies were grander than grand—but the smell of the food was making me salivate. There was nothing on the plates in front of the dollies. Of course not. No one wasted people food on dollies.

This girl was either teasing me or truly daft. "Does Alexandra really have a share?"

"Absolutely."

"Where?"

"Just take it. Off the serving plate."

A throbbing started in my temples. Her dolly actually had a share of this grand food. "How much?"

"However much you want."

It couldn't be true. No one was allowed to eat as much as they wanted.

I put a finger on the hare and looked at the girl. She was watching me, but she didn't stop me. I couldn't bear it a moment longer. I yanked a joint off and took a bite fast. The girl was still silent. I chewed. It was delicious. Dense and rich. Nearly as good as spuds. I ate and ate till there was nothing in my hand but two bones.

"You don't have the best etiquette."

"What's that?"

"Table manners. If you eat with your fingers, you should use only the first three."

I looked at my greasy fingers, then licked them.

She wrinkled her nose. "Clean up properly."

With what? I held my hand over the cover and looked at her. She frowned. My hand hovered over the lacy square cloth. She frowned again. Her eyes pointed toward a little folded cloth beside the dolly's plate. Amazing. I wiped my hand on that cloth. She nodded approval.

"That's a serviette," she said cheerily, but with a strange

precision, like people used when they talked with folk who had no brains. "It's what polite people use to wipe fingers and lips."

Polite people. Did she think she was polite? I stared at her. She stared back.

"So," I said, "what's your name?"

"Sue. But you should call me Miss Susanna."

"Why?"

"Long names feel more handsome."

"You don't need a long name," I said. "You are handsome."

"You think so? In what way?"

"You have pretty hair," I said.

"Ringlets." She brightened up and patted the bottom of her hair so it bounced. "I have so many ringlets. The hair-curling tongs make them." She smiled. "I curl Geraldine's hair too."

I smiled back. I couldn't help it; that's how I was built. And after all, she was talking to me at a normal pace again, not like I was a dunce. Maybe admiring her ringlets meant I'd passed her test for intelligence.

"So you liked the hare. Want to try the salmon?"

Salmon? There was only one other food on the table that I didn't recognize. It was pinkish and shiny, and it sat beside a plate of cookies. I nodded.

"Help yourself again. It was baked for the midday meal, but it's as cold as the hare now."

I grabbed a hunk of salmon before she could change her mind. My fingers went right through the flesh. I nibbled at it. It was delicious—a fantasy. I ate it all. Then I wiped my fingers carefully on the serviette.

"Well, at least you learn fast," said Miss Susanna. "But you have the strangest habits."

I blinked.

"Not just the way you eat. You dress as though the weather is hot. And your hair is a mess. You're plain old filthy."

I would normally have reacted to such an attack. To the stupidity of it—she actually thought I chose to have bare arms in this frigid air. I would have given her a tongue lash, I would, especially since I knew Ma would be mortified at what she'd said—even though I was in truth manky as a mudball, given all my tramping to the bog with Da. Oh, I would have, but my stomach had suddenly decided to flop around. I thought I might heave right there. I put my hands on my belly and leaned over my crossed legs.

"Your tummy hurts? You're not still hungry, are you?"

I shook my head.

"Good. Dad says all Irish exaggerate about being hungry. Even the prime minister says that. It was in the newspaper. Everyone knows you can always eat seaweed and field grasses if you want."

"We ate field grasses once last spring. We were sick for days after." The memory made me feel off-balance, as if I'd tip over if I weren't sitting. "You wouldn't know. You have everything."

"I don't have everything! That's a stupid thing to say! You have things I don't have."

"Like what?" I asked, but weakly. My heart wasn't in it. I felt too bad to really fight.

"You have tons of brothers and sisters. All Irish do."

"I don't."

"Oh." Miss Susanna gave a slight smile. "I better go back now."

I didn't ask where back was. My stomach was twisting like a live thing.

"Will you come again?"

I pressed both hands hard on my belly to stop the twisting.

"You will. Come soon." She set the serving plate on the ground. "Cook's going to be happy when she sees how much has been eaten. Dad made her promise to fatten me up." Then she collected the dollies' plates and the serviettes and stood. She carried them to a carriage that I hadn't noticed before. She folded the lacy white cloth and put it in the carriage. Then she put the three dollies in the carriage. "You have to stand, silly."

I blinked.

"How can I put the cover in my baby carriage if you're sitting on it?"

I managed to stand and step off the cover.

And now I realized Miss Susanna was taller than me. Just barely, but enough. And fatter, of course. She seemed powerful. She folded the cover and put it in the carriage. "When you come again, I'll bring more food. What would you like?"

Really? Maybe she wasn't so horrible after all. "Spuds."

"Well, I don't know what that is, but I'll ask Cook to make it. Come tomorrow."

"I will," I said. "I'll bring Paddy. He's my brother."

"You said you didn't have brothers and sisters."

"I don't. He's the only one. I'll bring him. I'll bring all of them. All my friends."

"No."

No? "Why not?"

"I said so."

What kind of answer was that? All haughty, like some sort of princess. But we needed that food. "Just the girls, then," I said as agreeably as I could. "And Paddy."

"No. How on earth could I control a pack of you?"

"We're not animals. We don't run in packs."

"You know what I meant."

I was sure I did. But I had to be careful and not say anything too harsh; I had to think of the food. "We're good girls. Grand, even. Deirdre would let you hold Nola, I bet. She's a baby. Her skin is so soft."

"No one. You have to come alone."

I looked at the serving dish, which was still sitting on the ground. "What are you going to do with the rest of that food?"

"You can't take it, if that's what you're thinking." She picked up the serving dish and put it into the baby carriage. "Pay attention. We need some rules. You must come alone. And you can't tell anyone about me. Those are the rules. That's all."

"You'd like Paddy." *Please,* I thought. *Paddy, at least.*

"If you show up with anyone else, I'll tell Dad. And he'll sic the dogs on you. He says you're all ragamuffins."

"You're not nice."

"I am too. You just don't know me well enough yet. I fed you, didn't I?"

My stomach wanted to empty. I clamped my lips shut hard.

"Come tomorrow and I'll have Cook make spuds and you'll see how nice I am."

I shook my head. "I can't come without Paddy. He's little. I have to take care of him."

"What about your nanny?"

"What?"

"Oh. Well. You don't have a nanny. I can see that. I don't have one right now myself. Dad fired my nanny and then I begged him to take me to Ireland with him, so he's not hiring a new one till I get back." She frowned. "Well, so, your brother needs care. But you came today without him."

"That was special."

"Well, surely you don't have to take care of him on Sunday. Even Catholics don't work on Sunday. Your parents can take care of him. So come on Sunday. That's not too long to wait. In the afternoon, like today. I'll bring the leftovers from our mid-day meal. It'll be better food than you've ever tasted."

I bristled, no matter that it was true. "How do you know that?"

"I'm not blind."

CHAPTER SEVEN

Indigestion

I groaned. My belly had been ruined by that feast. It was two days later, and I was still sick. At this rate, I'd fill the pit under our bog stool and Da would have to dig a new one. Normally he did that nasty job in summer. He'd be cranky about doing it when the cold ground was solid as rock.

I cleaned my bottom with a handful of mullein leaves from the pile. That pile would run out at this rate too. Then everyone would be cranky.

But the thing that would make them the crankiest would be finding out I ate that feast and didn't bring back anything for them—not a single bite. I walked slowly to our cottage, weighed down by this secret. I hated it.

And everyone was extra cranky these days, because every day either Da or Ma had missed a night of sleep. They were now taking turns guarding our kitchen garden at night. They'd been doing that ever since the beggar man put the idea into Ma's head that people might come in the night and steal our turnips.

"Lorraine!"

The sound came so sudden and sharp, I stumbled backward. "What, Ma?"

"Just look at you. My mind's already heavy with your da acting like he doesn't think straight anymore—I can't have you off wasting time, fussing about and getting nothing done. Not you too."

I never fooster over anything. Little Paddy does, not me. "I was only out back at the bog, Ma."

"Again?" She squinted at me. "You look like you didn't sleep a wink. Totally shattered."

I was. I wanted to drop onto the mat I shared with little Paddy and go right back to sleep.

"You're as bad off as Paddy. And here I was thinking you were stronger." Ma put her hand in her hair and shook her head sadly. "You're not eating enough, don't think I haven't noticed. You barely touched your food yesterday."

I would have laughed if my belly hadn't been cramping so hard. I'd eaten too much. It was the rest of them who hadn't eaten enough. And despite all that eating, I felt hungry again. That's how stomachs were. Greedy. Greedy and weak to temptation. What a bad person I was.

"Go get yourself ready and we're off to church. Praying is one thing we can do, at least."

Church? It was Sunday? So soon. I cringed. Miss Susanna had said to come back on Sunday. My jaw tightened. Miss Susanna had more food than she needed. But if I ate her food when everyone else was hungry, how could I face them? I couldn't let myself do it again. I wouldn't let myself think about Miss Susanna. I vowed never to visit her again.

I looked at Ma. She was tying on a bonnet, but her feet

were bare and they'd stay that way. Her shoes had worn away entirely. When? A long time ago now. And I had no shoes either. What did it mean to get ready for church, then? We had nothing to put on. But I didn't say that. And, of course, I did have a kerchief to cover my head with. At least I still had that.

I fought off the image of Miss Susanna's shoes. Her shawl. Her bonnet.

I went inside and tied my kerchief on. Then I searched all around our sleeping mat, all around Ma and Da's sleeping mat. I walked through the cottage, stepping everywhere, pushing things aside, including Muc, who squealed indignantly but obliged me by moving. Nothing there. I looked under the stool Da was sitting on. He was staring off into space.

"What are you doing?" Little Paddy sat on the dirt near the hearth playing with his stone collection. He had arranged them in a big circle with little circles inside. I didn't recognize the game.

"I'm looking for Margaret."

"Margaret? Oh, Margaret! Your dolly. I like her. She's nice."

"Where is she?"

"How should I know?"

"Where's who?" Ma stood in the doorway.

"Lorraine wants Margaret. Her dolly."

Ma's eyes clouded.

Da somehow came alert. "You're too old for a dolly."

"I am not."

"I say you are," he barked.

Why was Da being harsh? He was the one who made me

Margaret in the first place. From one of his old playing bones.

"Let her be, Francis," said Ma. "We could all use an extra friend these days. And I don't think Margaret's going to get any more use from anyone else. In fact, I hope not. We can't feed the mouths we already have." Ma went over to a high shelf and ran her fingers along it till she grabbed on to something. She handed me Margaret.

And I realized: I was holding the doll of the little sister I'd never have. So Da hadn't been acting harsh with me; he's been acting protective of Ma and that little sister.

I thought about baby Nola. Deirdre got to hold her almost all the time. She was a big-eyed, squirmy, and silent bundle. Every now and then Deirdre let me hold her. I loved her hot, milky breath. But I didn't really want a sister. I didn't. No more babies for us. I agreed with Ma. Hunger changed everything. I rubbed the dust off Margaret's funny face.

We walked across the land, the four of us, following a little country path, a boreen, out to the road, where the cottier families were waiting. We made a procession on the road toward town, the kids trampling the grass strip in the middle, where the wagon wheels didn't go. It was mostly downhill and the sea breeze actually brought a little relief from the cold today. I could move my free hand from rubbing my arm to rubbing that cramping belly.

"What's the matter with you?" asked Fiona.

"I ate too much."

Fiona laughed. "That's not really funny, though, you know. Remember the days when we could really get full? The good old days." She laughed again.

Iona wriggled in between us and reached up to touch my doll. She poked her fingers in Margaret's eyes and mouth. She rubbed Margaret's nose gently.

"Look!" shouted Corey.

"Oh no!" screamed Deirdre.

Suddenly everyone was crowding forward to see, then crying out, saying, *how awful, how sad, how revolting*.

Little Paddy grabbed my hand. I tried to free myself, but he clutched even tighter. Well, I wasn't about to be left out, so if whatever they were shouting about was really bad, he'd just have to see it. I pushed my way forward with little Paddy clinging to me.

And there they were: the man and his snappers. The ones that had come the other day, before I went out and gathered wild celery and watercress. Before I met Miss Susanna. Just a few days ago. My whole face stung and I could hardly see for a moment. It was as though a giant bee was buzzing around inside my head. They were lying dead on the road. I'd never seen people dead on the road before. I'd only seen one dead person who wasn't yet in a casket—my granny. These people looked much worse than Granny had, though. She'd been dead on her sleeping mat, with a serene face. But their faces showed nothing. They seemed to have just lain down and waited for death together with no more feelings than tree branches. They didn't seem like people at all. They were as different from Granny as the moon was from the sun; they looked like no one had ever loved them. I could hear a constant whimper.

And, oh no, where was the third child?

"God's will," said Fiona's da. He stood over the bodies, intoning like our priest sometimes did. Then he picked up Aeden and his hand cupped the little boy's head like a cap, like our da did to little Paddy. "We should bury them."

"No," said Ma. "Don't touch them. It's not safe."

"But they can't just stay here like this," said Fiona's ma. "Dogs . . ." She stopped and looked around at us kids, then moved closer to Ma. "You know. We can't leave them. They deserve a proper burial."

"They'll get it," said Emmet's da. "Maybe not proper, but a burial, at least. Soldiers will come and take them away."

"How do you know that?" asked Fiona's ma.

"It's what they've been doing. These aren't the only dead bodies by the roadside." Emmet's da shook his head. "Leave it to the soldiers."

"Food for worms," said Emmet under his breath.

I moved away from Emmet and stared harder at the bodies. I couldn't see any worms. And that whimper was getting louder.

Where, oh where, was that third child?

But another set of screams had already started. The third body was off in the grasses.

"Something ate his legs!"

"A dog. Like my ma said. She's always warning us. She calls those packs ravenous. They're dangerous."

I looked around. Were the dogs still nearby, lurking? Would they come at us? I tucked Margaret inside my bodice and put my hands over little Paddy's ears and pulled him to me.

"I saw them before," said little Paddy. His eyes brimmed with tears. He took my hands off his ears and clutched them hard. "They were outside our home, that man and those children."

"That's nothing," said Riley. "They spent the night in our home."

Ma was by my side again now, her hand on my shoulder. At Riley's words, she squeezed so hard I had to bite my lip to keep from yelping. "Your ma let them inside?"

"It's what you're supposed to do," said Deirdre. "There's always enough for one more."

"That's true of food. You can keep dividing it. But . . ." Ma pressed her lips together. "Ah, well, it doesn't matter at this point."

"What doesn't matter?" said Quinlin. "Are you saying it was wrong to let them in?"

"I spoke out of turn," said Ma.

The ma of Deirdre and Quinlin and Riley and baby Nola came up behind Ma. "Let's go off and talk, Catherine." She took Ma by the arm, but Ma pulled herself free—not mean-like, just firm. They walked back up the road together, the way we'd come. Their heads bent forward, bobbing; their shoulders said they were arguing.

And that whimpering I heard, it just wouldn't stop. It filled my head.

"This is what it's come to," said Alana's ma. "This is worse than ever. And winter's still ahead, just a couple of weeks off." She shook her head. "Let's get going. Church is waiting."

"What's the point of going to church?" said Alana's da.

"What?" Alana's ma looked shocked. "What's gotten into you?"

"We don't even have a proper place to hold service anyway. We need a true stone building, with a slate roof above our heads, like in the big towns. Or even a thatched cottage, like in some of the other small towns—that could do us. But we Catholics stand out in the open while the others get the real church. It isn't right."

"At least the children get Sunday school," said Alana's ma.

"A half hour with the nuns telling them things that will never matter to them anyway. What good is that?"

"It's better than nothing. And I like the sky overhead. It's heaven, after all."

"You know what we really need?" said Da. "*Saoirse*—freedom. We need the freedom of heaven above us, we do. But we need freedom below us too. We shouldn't have to spend all our time standing on land that belongs to others. Let's do our own kind of church today. Let's go to the shore."

"That's a good idea, Francis," said Ma, coming back down the road. "Let's breathe the fresh air and wash ourselves with the salt water."

"We'll freeze to death," said Alana's ma.

Ma pursed her lips and she looked hard at Alana's ma, as though her eyes were trying to speak. "Not if we rub ourselves hard. We can scour ourselves. It'll cleanse us the right way." Her voice shook a little, like when little Paddy or I had done something bold. But I didn't know why she'd feel like that now. "We can get clean and pray together on our own today. Just us—just us five families."

"You go," said Teagan's ma. "But we won't. We'll go on into town, our family. We won't leave the priest waiting."

"He's got plenty of others to tend to," said Ma. "But you go if you want. We'll each do what we need to do today."

So the rest of us cut west, along the path through the tufts of tall grasses, out to the white, sandy strand. And there was the sea. Close to us it was light as Ma's eyes and then darker and darker as we looked further out. Stretching forever. Vast.

Minutes later we saw a dolphin jump. Then another. And another. They seemed joyous. And out there—how far? maybe two hundred feet—was a sandbar with seals. Black and dark brown and gray and silver and stark white. The whole gamut of colors. And, oh, many of them were pups, forming high white piles! I loved those short snouts and round faces. I loved the down-and-up slants of their nostrils. I loved everything about them. I wanted to be in one of those piles with them. I wanted all of us to be in those piles.

We stripped and ran into the sea and screamed at how cold it was. Like I imagined knives would be, lashing at our chests and backs, making us shake everywhere. Then we ran back to the sand and our mas enveloped us in their skirts.

Ma rubbed so hard, I thought my very skin would come off. But I didn't cry now and I didn't even scream. Neither did little Paddy. Ma's face showed she meant business. Her hands worked in desperation and her teeth clenched.

Then Ma pulled little Paddy and me to her chest so tight, I

had to fight to breathe. I kept thinking of the seal pups. Funny little pups. Did they have to fight to breathe, the ones on the bottom of those piles?

But even if they did, they made me happy. Teeth-chatteringly happy.

Still, I couldn't stop clutching Margaret.

And I couldn't stop whimpering.

CHAPTER EIGHT

Petals

The week had passed in a blur of cold mud and punishing winds. We even had a snowfall on the eleventh of December—so beautiful I would have loved it if I'd had a jumper and shoes. It was Sunday again, finally, and we were gathered out in the open listening to the priest. I was glad to be there. I'd been afraid Ma and Da would insist on going to the strand again, and I couldn't bear the thought of that freezing water in these new, more horrid winds. It was bad enough last time, but if we'd gone today, I was sure we'd have perished right there on the sands. So I looked at the priest with gratitude.

He stood on a low stone platform. The rest of us stood on the cold damp ground at the bottom of Main Street. Or most of the rest of us did. Some hadn't shown up for mass. Maybe they had gone to the strand again. If so, I hoped they were looking at dolphins now. At least they should have that pleasure. And I prayed they weren't fools enough to stray into the water.

Ma and Da looked attentive, nodding at the priest's words. They'd been sleeping good again, because the harsh cold had made them pull all the rest of the turnip harvest and store it in the corner of our cottage farthest from the hearth, so there was nothing left to guard at night. No one would steal frostbite kale or cabbage; it was simply too much work to hike all the way to our cottage for food that couldn't sustain anyone. So Ma and Da had the energy to listen now.

I tried to be attentive to the priest too. He spoke loud and firm, telling us suffering had a purpose. Jesus had suffered. Now it was our turn. We had to hold on, keep the faith that things would get better. This was a test. Every day was a test. We'd make it through the winter, and, sure as anything, spring would come and the earth would provide again. God would provide. We must accept that. We must keep the faith.

And most of all, we must not fall prey to the Protestant ministers who called this a "favorable crisis"—evidence that God wanted us to turn away from Catholicism. They called Catholicism "the huge darkness." But they were wrong. Our faith was the very definition of light. The fact that they could look at the peasantry's disaster—our disaster—as an opportunity to make their church prosper showed how far they had strayed from the light. There was no time ever in history when it was more important to keep the faith.

The words came like a distant drum. I heard them. I knew the language they were spoken in. I believed them—I was a good Catholic girl, I loved my faith. But still, those words felt like they weren't really talking to me. Ma's voice played in my head instead, singing, *"Hear the wind blow, love, hear the wind blow. Lean your head over and hear the wind blow."* But that singing ma in my head was wrong. She'd said herself that you couldn't eat the view. Well, you couldn't eat the wind, either.

And you couldn't eat faith.

My eyes wandered away from the priest and searched the woodland opposite from where we stood. The graveyard there had fresh plots all in a row. That was because tuberculosis was on the rise again, like last winter. It had raged through a farm to the south of here and no one in our congregation would stand near the survivors. Not yet, at least. Birds hopped around on the surface of those graves. I didn't want to remember Emmet's words—*food for worms*—but I did. So now I imagined worms in the graveyard. How did worms manage in this frozen-hard dirt?

Was anyone managing in Ireland these days? Anyone other than the English?

Finally, the priest blessed the congregation and two nuns took us children aside to talk about sound morals. They said in times like these one might think that all that mattered was finding a scrap to eat, a shawl to throw across our shoulders. But we mustn't forget that how we treated one another was important, keeping our dignity was important, maybe more important than when times were good. I believed those words too—just as I believed the priest's words. How could they be wrong, after all? I listened hard. These were words I could tuck into my heart. The nuns talked about civility, about keeping up the habits that allowed humans to remember they were the children of God. But then they gave examples, and, oh, it seemed that good manners and a respectable appearance were important supports of sound morals and that ever-important civility.

Anger pricked at my insides. I was surprised at how much

it smarted. Good manners? I wasn't really sure what good manners were anymore. We hardly ever socialized with anyone. And, oh, what a lot of voices there were inside my head today, for I could hear Miss Susanna criticizing my table manners. The girl who put food on her dollies' plates while we were so hungry—that girl had the nerve to talk about manners.

And a respectable appearance—those words meant nothing anymore. Miss Susanna, dressed all frilly with shoes and bonnet, had called me filthy. Well, I'd wear anything, no matter how ragged or dirty, if it could keep me warm. What good was looking respectable if you were frozen to death?

So I didn't want to hear any more from these nuns. I was ready to walk away, but—what was this? They promised we'd have a celebration with a parade through the town streets on Saint Brigid's Day, the first of February. And they were planning a Whitsun outing after Easter. I used to love outings, though now I couldn't imagine finding the energy to go on one. But a short parade, that would be lovely. Maybe they'd give us costumes to wear. Warm costumes. If we could just make it to February, maybe we'd have something warm to put on.

At last the nuns hushed. We turned to our mas and das and promised to stick together. We promised to shout loud if a dog came up. We promised to find a place to talk and then return home before dark, staying on the well-traveled boreens we knew so well. We promised and promised, until our mas and das finally gave permission for us to walk the narrow, crooked road that was Bridge Street.

We moved as a unit; we'd have been shoulder to shoulder if

we'd all been the same height. We passed the graveyard and all of us sang softly. And we kept singing as we went by the gaol. A soldier in uniform and carrying a rifle went in through the front door. I'd never seen soldiers before this winter. People said they were here to maintain order, because the workhouses were overcrowded and the people they turned away could get violent. And, of course, I knew now that they were here to scoop up the dead by the roadside.

"Scared, are you?" said a man sitting out front, which was, of course, why we sang. Anyone in their right mind sang passing those places.

"Nothing scares me," said Emmet.

I looked fast at him. The fibber.

"Then you're a fool." The man smiled with rotted teeth. "Patt Flanagan stole a watch. You won't see him for seven years. Transported he'll be. And James Wade, two months' hard labor for stealing a pig."

I didn't know people were stealing pigs. I thought of Muc and squeezed little Paddy's hand. We'd freeze at night without our pig. Truly freeze.

"Ah," said the rotten-toothed man, pointing at me. "Do you think you'd be spared, little lady, just because you're a girl? Think again. Margaret Rabbit got three months' hard labor for larceny. And that fancy Catherine Halloran, well, six months for her."

At the name Margaret, I thought of my bone dolly. I'd left her at home, because I realized last week that Iona coveted her. It wasn't nice to show off—it was better to be empty-handed.

I'd been taking Margaret on my chores all week, so it felt strange to be without her today. But now I had another reason to be glad I'd left her home: She didn't have to hear about this other, disreputable Margaret—the one who was off doing hard labor. I didn't know what the other Margaret had done, but the sound of the new word this man used hurt my ears. I moved farther away from him.

Emmet looked at me, and abruptly he spoke: "None of us steals." How funny, he was defending me. He might be a fibber, but he wasn't a horrible boy after all. I wanted to hug him, but I knew he'd never let me. "And none of us does that larceny thing, whatever it is."

I looked at Emmet with admiration: He'd picked up that word just like that. *Larceny.* Emmet was smart.

"Pranks get punished too," said the man. "In the next sessions there's a young gentleman to be tried for throwing an oyster shell at Miss Chalmers while she was on the stage."

"Come along." Alana grabbed Emmet by the elbow.

"But smile at him politely," said Noreen. "Remember what the nuns said. Good manners, everyone." And the tone of her voice told me she was saying it tongue in cheek. She was cross at the nuns too.

My insides smarted again. But it wasn't anger at the nuns this time. And it wasn't anger at this man with the rotted teeth either. It was just anger.

Still, I did what everyone else did: We all threw the nasty man a forced smile and turned our faces down as we raced past the courthouse, half to escape him and half just to arrive at our goal. That goal was the harbor, and I couldn't wait. The sight of that wide expanse of water was like a charm. It wasn't as wild as the open sea, but its calm was far better right now; the harbor was protected from the worst winds. That was reassuring, and I sensed we could all use strong reassurance, the undeniable kind that only nature gave.

The road ended and we walked along the stream. The water was turf brown. It foamed as it went through the series of little cascades. I liked the sound of it, even though it made me shiver harder.

"A salmon!" Corey pointed in one of the slow-turning pools at the bottom of a cascade.

At his words, it was as though a fish flipped in my stomach. I'd eaten salmon . . . with Miss Susanna in the woods. My awful secret made my cheeks flame up through my ears.

Emmet ran to Corey's side and squinted into the dark swirls. "Oh, there he is! Catch him."

"With what?"

"Don't ask me. You're the one who saw him."

"You don't know anything about fishing," said Corey. "Admit it. You couldn't catch a dead fish if it floated under your nose."

"Nobody's doing any catching," said Alana. She put her hand on Emmet's chest as if to hold him back.

"But they're good eating."

"What a story! You've never tasted salmon."

"I've heard. Everyone says."

"It's illegal," said Fiona.

"Can't be," said Emmet. "Fish don't belong to anyone."

"You don't know," said Teagan. "A woman was down at the rocks gathering cockles and limpets, and a landlord sent a man with a gun to scare her off. Said that part of the shore belonged to him. I heard someone talking with my da and he was witness to it. My da knows everything about the law."

"Real fish are different from shellfish," said Emmet. "They swim everywhere. And the sea doesn't belong to anyone. No one's that rich."

"You're just wrong, Emmet," said Noreen. "Like Teagan said, our da knows the law. He says if it were legal to kill the sea life, we'd all be eating those seal pups."

"Who cares?" Emmet threw up his hands. "Let's catch the salmon."

Alana shook her head. "We'd need a net, or a pole and hook, or something, anyway. It isn't that easy or our das would be here every night trying to snag dinner."

"Some dinner," said Fiona. "One fish for all of us."

"I'd be glad for a single bite," said Neil.

Everyone was silent for a moment. I bet they were wondering what salmon tasted like, thinking of something new on their tongue—something that might be as substantial as spuds. And it was. The memory left me breathless.

As though a silent message had passed among us, we stopped and huddled together, with the littler ones pressed into the center. The harbor now seemed far away.

Little Aeden tugged on Fiona's dress. "Is it time yet?"

"I don't know." Fiona looked across us.

"This is as good a spot as any," I said.

"Do we start with the telling or the giving?"

"The telling," said Murray. "If I'm not chosen for the giving, I want to leave fast and not watch."

"Me too," said Kyla. "So who's telling?"

"It was supposed to be Riley," said Emmet.

Everyone went silent.

"Where is Riley?" asked little Paddy.

The others exchanged glances. They had a secret. What?

Then I made a full inventory. I went a little quivery in my stomach. "Where are all of them?" I asked. "Riley and Quinlin and Deirdre and baby Nola." I looked from face to face. "And their ma and da. The whole family. They didn't come to church."

No one answered. Some looked away. They knew something.

I made my voice firm, though the quiver inside me grew. "Where did the family go? Tell."

"They have the fever," said Fiona, at last.

"What fever?"

"The one that kills."

"Don't say that!" Emmet pushed Fiona. "Don't ever say that."

Alana put her arm around Emmet from behind and pulled him to her. He wrestled free, his face blotched red and white. "Emmet's right." Alana folded her hands. "Let's all pray."

"To a saint," said Carrick. "One of our saints."

"Saint Macdara," said Kyla.

"Are you kidding? That feast isn't till July. Saint Féichín's feast is in January . . . so it's almost time."

And so we said a silent prayer to Saint Féichín, and I pressed against little Paddy.

"Now let's curse," said Emmet.

Fiona's eyes flashed. "Are you gone in the head?"

"It's what my da does," said Emmet. "Nothing works better than singing, praying, and mourning in Irish. Nothing but cursing in Irish. That's what he says. And we've already done the singing and praying."

"Works better at what?" asked Fiona.

"Just works better," said Emmet. "That's all. Just works better."

"Do it silently, then," said Fiona. "My da gets cross when he hears cursing."

"He couldn't hear us from way out here."

"Do it silently anyway," said Fiona.

So we all cursed silently in Irish.

"And we should visit a holy well," said Neil.

"Who knows where a holy well is, Neil?" Murray punched his brother in the shoulder.

"It's time, then, let's do the telling." Fiona looked around. "Who's our volunteer?"

"Me." Teagan nodded.

"And you have to do it in English," said Kearney. "Remember?"

We'd agreed to do our tellings in English. To practice. Because in America people spoke English . . . and these days more and more Irish families were getting on ships and going to Canada and from there to America, where everyone had plenty of food. None of our mas and das were talking about getting on a ship—not yet, at least. Who had the money for tickets? Which was just as well, because every Irish person alive had a fisherman relative who'd been lost in the depths. The sea could be treacherous. Staying might turn out even more treacherous, though. We kids had decided it was best to be ready.

"I remember, I do," said Teagan, in an English sweetened by a quick Irish tongue and just the smallest trace of something else—maybe her first mother's Welsh. "I've been planning this, practicing. And the recipe took a lot of thinking, a lot of searching my memory from when I was little, with my first family. I'm pretty sure I have it right—both what I'm going to say and how I'm going to say it. So listen." She held her hands out, just like our priest did when he wanted us to listen. "You need a sharp cheese. Cheddar is best. Good Welsh cheddar."

"I've never tasted it," said Kearney.

"You will now. Shut your eyes. Go on, now—shut them tight. This cheese, it's firm, but not hard. You have to press down, but then your teeth sink in slow. It's creamy, but . . . oh, I don't know how to say it in English."

"Then say it in Irish," said someone.

"It's not the kind of cream that comes up with a mere flick of the tongue," said Teagan in Irish. "You have to lick and lick it. It would take hundreds of licks to eat it. So you don't really lick it."

"I want to lick it," said Kearney.

"Hush, Kearney," said someone, and I was sure it was Alana.

"It's allowed," said Teagan. "You can lick it if you want. Now you grate that cheese and add butter and milk and chopped mustard. Can you smell it? Does your nose itch inside?"

"Mine does," said someone—probably Noreen. But I knew it was true, because my nose itched inside too.

"Good."

"Switch back to English," said someone.

"Now you add Worcestershire sauce," said Teagan in English. "And don't ask what it is, because I don't know the Irish word. It's brown and sharp from vinegar but sweet from molasses, and it's the best thing in the world. So you heat it all with pepper and salt till it's like smooth cream, and you pour it over toast and then bake it."

"You cook it twice?"

"Twice. Once in the pot and once in the oven. And it's just so good. You have to wait, to make sure it won't burn you. . . ."

Someone clapped. "Like with spuds."

"That's right. But you wait only a little bit, because it's important to gobble it down before it's cool."

"You can't say 'gobble,'" said someone. "That's an Irish word."

"It's Irish and it's English at the same time," said Teagan. "It's even Welsh."

"Maybe it's every language," said someone.

"It's not. My da told me."

"Gobble gobble gobble," said someone softly.

"Gobble gobble." And soon everyone was saying, "Gobble." We said it over and over till we were all laughing.

"That was a good telling, Teagan," said Emmet.

"Well, now," said Murray, shifting back to Irish. "Who gets the giving?"

This was the first time we'd done a giving. It had been Deirdre's idea, because with each passing week the telling seemed to satisfy less—we needed something more. Cunning Deirdre, and now she wasn't even here to be part of it.

"How do we choose?" said little Paddy.

I hadn't thought of that. From the looks on the others' faces, I could tell they hadn't either. Maybe Deirdre had devised a plan, but it looked like she hadn't told anyone. "I'll choose," I blurted out.

"You can't choose," said Murray. "You'll choose yourself."

I shook my head hard. I'd never choose myself.

"Or Paddy," said Fiona.

"Fair. I'll do it fair." I stared at them hard, each in turn. "Everyone can hold out their hands, and I'll shut my eyes and feel the tips and just stop at someone."

"Then you can't be the one who gets it," said little Paddy. "You'll be left out. That's not fair."

"I don't care. I don't want it." And I didn't. It would be wonderful. But I didn't deserve it . . . not after having that feast in the woods that day. Being left out now would offer the beginning of atonement. Good.

"What if you know whose hand it is?" said Noreen. She shook her head. "I think we should all go pick a leaf and hide it.

You know, cover it up. Then the one who picked one that's most like the one Lorraine picked will win."

We nodded, then quietly scattered. Winter leaves were everywhere. I squatted in the middle of a patch of plants, shut my eyes, and picked one at random. I opened my eyes. It wasn't a leaf at all—it was a purple petal from a sweet coltsfoot. A pretty little thing, all fragile. It smelled like vanilla. I loved winter wildflowers, and sweet coltsfoot was my favorite. I put it on one palm and quick cupped the other over it so no one could see. Then I stood and went back to our original spot and waited.

Everyone came back with hands cupped just like mine. I had expected them to squabble—at least the boys—but they just looked big-eyed at one another and didn't say a word. I held out my hands, then opened them. Everyone opened their hands. Green leaves of many types. But Carrick had a groundsel petal. "Carrick," I said.

I expected someone to object that Carrick's was yellow, while mine was purple. I expected someone to object that petals weren't really leaves. I expected someone to cry. But no one did any of that.

We all handed over our tiny and precious gifts from pockets and wherever else we'd been storing them. A dried berry. A sliver of onion. A shriveled mushroom. Bits of food—just one bite's worth. Carrick would get to eat them all.

And for a moment maybe, just maybe, he'd feel full.

CHAPTER NINE

Nola

"Where are you going?"

Little Paddy stopped and looked back at me. "Nowhere."

"You can't walk and go nowhere."

"You go off and do whatever you want all the time," said little Paddy. He flicked his hand at me like Da sometimes did when I annoyed him. "You're busy. Go. I'm busy too." He turned and walked slowly off.

I wasn't busy. Not anymore. All the chores were done. I had gathered the holly boughs—the best kind, with bright red berries—days ago. I'd helped Ma make the wreath that hung on our front door. Da had made the traditional crib to put near the front door, and I was the one to decorate it. I had gone searching and found ivy with bunches of purple berries. All those winter berries had no right to look so juicy, given that they were so poisonous, but at least their beauty would grace our home. I wove the ivy in and out the side sticks of the crib and frosted the berries with a cream made of starch and water. And just the day before, I'd helped Da clean out the chimney. Our cottage was ready for the holiday.

There was nothing left to do. Or nothing I would have any

part in. Da would take care of finding the big Yule log. And Ma would do the cooking, whatever that meant.

But really, deep inside me I hoped it meant something good. Maybe Da or Ma or both of them had a surprise saved up for the holiday. It was possible. After all, if we kids could scrape together morsels for a giving, Ma and Da could come up with something that surprised little Paddy and me. They could. It was possible.

I coughed. The corners of my mouth cracked. My skin was so dry, even a cough could tear it. Little Paddy's skin was dry too; his hands flaked. Now I watched his wing bones poking out against the back of his shirt, till he disappeared behind hedges. Ma and Da were off somewhere, and though Christmas was any day now, I suspected it had nothing to do with that. I was anxious about them. Their faces had been grim when they left. I was anxious about all of us.

Keep the faith.

The cold was bad and getting worse each day. I thought of the fever hut—that's what we were all calling Deirdre's family's hut. Ma knew more about fever than anyone could ever want; her parents and sisters had all died of it when she was just a little older than I was now. So she had made the rules and all of us obeyed: We weren't allowed to go near the fever hut and they weren't allowed to come out. I didn't want a fever, of course not—but I kept thinking maybe they were lucky to have fever right now. I couldn't remember winter ever being this cold before.

I walked back inside our cottage and picked up Margaret.

She looked the same as always. I shook her. She was silent.

I walked over to Muc, who was asleep. I sighed dramatically. Muc didn't stir.

A silent bone and a sleeping pig.

I put Margaret back on the sleeping mat and walked outside, in the direction little Paddy had gone. He hadn't told me not to follow, after all.

He wasn't hard to find; he was sitting near a hedge, crooning to something in his hands. I craned my neck. Why, it was a hedgehog. That darling baby, I guessed, the one he had named Pointy. And it was now twice the size it had been when Da caught it. Which meant it was still very small, that's how these creatures were, but, oh glory, how it had grown. I gaped. Somehow little Paddy had managed to tame it, a remarkable feat, since I was pretty sure hedgehogs curled away somewhere for the winter. We never saw them when the ground was cold. Little Paddy had a way with animals. I guess I'd always known that, but I didn't like to think about it too much. I didn't have a way with anything. He was patient; I wasn't. Maybe it took patience to get good at anything.

Little Paddy laughed and chattered away at the animal. It had been a long time since I'd heard him laugh. Nothing in our home these days excited a laugh. I was tempted to join them. I wanted to laugh too. But it might ruin it for him. This was his treat. And he'd earned it, with all his hard work of training the creature.

I snuck away, toward our cottage again, because I couldn't think where else to go. We weren't supposed to stray this morning, though no one had explained why. Maybe I could get Muc to chase me around the outside of the cottage. She used to do that when she was young. She used to be the best piglet ever. But she'd never want to run now. In truth, I didn't think I could manage a run either.

I was coming up behind the cottage when I heard Ma and Da on the other side.

"Poor Nola. Poor, poor baby."

"Stop saying that, Catherine. It doesn't change anything."

"I keep thinking about her ma, losing such a babe—such a tiny one. I couldn't bear it."

"You could bear it. You would. And she will. Everyone's bearing that kind of loss, everywhere you turn."

"But baby Nola. The sweetest ever."

"Hush, I said. She'll bear it. And she'll bear losing all the rest of her babes too. She shouldn't have let those folk in her home. You said it yourself. I'm glad you were cunning. We're safe, at least. We're not losing anyone."

My ears felt like when I dunked myself underwater, like the water was locking all this noise inside my head. I came around the cottage. "Losing?" I said. "What do you mean?" I knew what Da meant, though. Still, I prayed he'd tell me I was wrong.

"Lorraine!" Ma's face went blotchy as though someone had belted her. "You look a sight. Do you have the fever?" She rushed over and put the back of her hand to my forehead. Lately she was in the habit of doing that several times a day.

I stepped away. "I'm healthy, Ma." I gulped the air and

forced myself to ask. "Did baby Nola die?" My own words felt unreal to me.

"Come inside, by the fire." Ma shooed me in through the door.

I moved like nothing—like I was empty skin—lighter than the air. "Tell me."

Ma went over to my sleeping mat and picked up Margaret. She smoothed her with one hand, then stopped and stared at her. "Nothing but a bone, really."

This was like Sunday, when everyone else knew something I didn't know and no one was letting me in on it. My head pressed tight from the inside so hard, I could barely see straight. If Da hadn't been there, I might have screamed, really screamed. "Tell me."

"Still, you shouldn't leave her on the mat," Ma said in a drifty kind of way. "All lonely. Poor Margaret." Ma's face went still.

"Tell me. Did she die?"

"She did." Da stepped close to me. His hand came down soft on my shoulder, then stayed like a heavy lump. "Baby Nola died last night."

The words had a life all their own. They sat on my head and weighed me down much more than Da's hand. Now they slid down the front of my face, cutting off my breath. Then down to my chest. My heart had to fight to beat.

"From the fever? The one that killed that man and his children?"

Da nodded.

I felt my lips moving. "What about the others? What about Deirdre and Quinlin and Riley?"

"They all have the fever."

"But will they die?"

"No one knows," said Ma, coming back to life.

"Da said they would. I heard. He said their ma will lose all of them."

"Da doesn't know," said Ma. "Only God knows. Look at me. I lived when everyone else in my family died. It's up to God."

Keep the faith. Faith meant acceptance. Acceptance felt beyond me.

There had to be some reason for it all. How did it happen? But I knew the answer to that, too. "It was the beggar man, wasn't it? The one with the children."

"Beggars are rife with the lice that carry black fever."

"That's why you made them stay outside, far from our cottage." My ma was cunning. Like Da said. I should be grateful. I was. But I still wanted to scream.

"At least it's a faster death than starvation," said Da.

Starvation. He'd said the word I hated so much. It felt like a blasphemy. It was all-powerful—worse than the devil himself. In its face, we were helpless. I couldn't bear to be helpless.

Starvation.

Did it really lie ahead? It hadn't looked so horrible on Granny's face. But maybe she had decided not to show it. That would have been like her.

Who says fibs are wrong?

My hands curled into fists. I refused to be helpless. I went out the door.

"Where are you going?" called Ma.

But I didn't look back. They wouldn't follow me. What would be the point? Besides, they didn't have the energy. No one had the energy for anything extra. But what I was doing now wasn't extra—I had to have the energy. I moved as fast as I could.

"Don't go near the others." Ma was shouting now. "It's not safe. Not till the fever runs its course."

Ah. So they really might follow me—they might waste what little energy they had. I couldn't allow that. And I couldn't put Ma through that worry. I stopped and turned.

Da was many steps behind me. He stopped when I did. I could hear his panting, even from here.

"I won't go near them," I said loud enough for him to hear. "I won't go near any of them. I promise."

Da looked at me and nodded. I could tell he was relieved he didn't have to catch me. He let his head drop, then turned and went back to the cottage.

It was a long walk to the base of the hill. Longer than last time. Long enough for shock to turn to sorrow. Words etched themselves in my brain: *Baby Nola shouldn't have died.*

The hill seemed steeper. The sharp rocks hurt the underside of my feet, and the ground was tricky—I nearly fell a few times. I had to be careful; hazel scrub could hide the entrance to a deep cave, and if I landed inside one, how would I find the strength to climb out?

The wind was mild, and I was glad for that. But still, I thought longingly of my old jumper. Next time I'd wear it. Ma hardly looked at me these days, after all. Fatigue blotted out anything but the necessities. Ma wouldn't even notice it was too small for me now.

The little stream where the watercress had grown was nothing but a twisty line of mud that cracked rather than squished. I didn't waste time searching for cress. Cress couldn't stave off starvation.

Starvation. That really was the key to it all. If they hadn't been starving, the beggar and his waifs wouldn't have come to us. The fever wouldn't have spread.

And now sorrow turned to anger. *Baby Nola shouldn't have died.*

By the time I reached the top of the hill, I felt light-headed. Dizzy almost. I didn't turn around to look toward the islands or the phantom cliffs. I couldn't risk doing anything extra.

Nothing ahead looked familiar. I wasn't sure which path I'd taken last time. Still, the castle had to be off to the right, no? That was south. It had to be south. Only, my brain wasn't working like it should. And I felt vaguely worried at how much time all this was taking. I ran and stumbled and ran again. A floppy run, as though my arms and legs weren't attached right. But it seemed running was called for, as though running was easier than walking when you went downhill, as easy as falling.

And fury was propelling me forward now. *Baby Nola shouldn't have died.*

Finally, the grove of trees appeared. They seemed skinnier

than last time. Absolutely bare of every last leaf. Who would have a party with her dollies among those bleak trees? No one. Miss Susanna wouldn't be there. She couldn't be. It wouldn't make sense.

I walked slowly now. I didn't want to see that there was no one among the trees. I didn't want to hear the silence.

I got to a place where the ground was level. The brown grasses were flattened. This was where Miss Susanna had spread her cover. She must have come recently, because grasses didn't stay flattened. Not even dead grasses. Birds and squirrels and mice—wind, too—lots of things would disturb the grasses and push them up again. So she was here not long ago. But she wasn't here now.

I fell to my knees. A small stick split under me with a sharp crack. It didn't even hurt. I realized I was half-numb. Maybe because of the cold. I felt like nothing could hurt me ever again. I dropped onto my bottom.

The cracked stick was white as bone. I picked it up and turned it in my hands. Where had all my fury fled to? I felt dead inside.

Baby Nola was dead. Inside and outside. She wouldn't squirm ever again. Her breath wasn't hot anymore. Deirdre's arms must have felt so useless. Like frayed old ropes. My own arms ached. Deirdre must have been crying right then. My eyes were dry, but I felt like my whole body was crying.

Or maybe Deirdre couldn't feel sad. Maybe she was numb, totally numb, much more numb than I was. Probably she was looking at Quinlin. And at Riley. With hot, dry eyes. Fever eyes.

She was their big sister, and still, she couldn't protect them. She was dying too.

I stretched out on my back and looked through the crisscrossing branches to the blue sky. Why did everything look so normal, so beautiful, when it was all so wrong?

I touched my cheeks and neck to be sure I was real. I squeezed my own shoulders. A wind started up now, colder than ever. A diabolical wind. An insistent wind. Like in songs. *Oh, winds that bring night,* I thought, *may your fury be crossed.*

This had to change. I refused to be like Deirdre. I couldn't endure that. I'd protect little Paddy, I would.

And I knew how. I'd come this far. I wouldn't stop now.

I stood up. I combed my fingers through my hair. I plucked dried twigs and grasses from my arms and legs. I brushed off my dress. There was nothing else I could do to make myself look better, more presentable, more respectable, as the nuns had said. So I'd just have to speak clear, slow English and stand up tall, so they'd listen. They had to listen. *Baby Nola shouldn't have died.*

All at once I remembered Miss Susanna saying her da would sic the dogs on me. I used to like dogs, way back when. But now they struck terror in my heart.

This wasn't a moment to give in, though. I stiffened up and walked through the trees in the direction of the castle. And as I stepped out of the trees, I saw her.

Miss Susanna was pushing her dolly carriage through the grasses toward me. She was still far off, but our eyes met. Hers panicked. She looked over her shoulder quick, then motioned to me to go back among the trees.

CHAPTER TEN

Temptation

W hy'd you come out of the trees?" Miss Susanna put her hands on her hips and her voice was a scold. "I saw you from the window, you know. I saw you and I made up an excuse to have my outing early, so Cook would quick put everything together for me. I rushed as fast as I could. And there you go, showing yourself, like some sort of idiot." She shook her head in disgust. "You have no idea how lucky you are that our housekeeper here is a dunce. Our housekeeper in England would have spotted you in an instant. Dad says she has an eye like a hawk. She would have run you off." She looked me up and down. "You look awful. A shabby thing. Shabby and daft."

I swallowed. "You look clean and well-fed." But that wasn't enough. She had to pay attention to me. I stuck my face in hers. "A spoiled thing."

Miss Susanna bunched up her cheeks and narrowed her eyes, and even her forehead turned red. "So you don't come back for how long? It'll be two full weeks tomorrow. Do you realize that? So you come at last, and then here you are, being a beast. That's not friendly."

"You started it."

Miss Susanna lifted her chin. "I am definitely not spoiled."

"You have plenty to eat. We have nearly nothing to eat."

"Exaggeration! Like Dad said. That's what all you Irish do. There's plenty for everyone here."

I shook my head. "Not in our home."

"Whose fault is that?" Miss Susanna turned her back and took the cover out of the dolly carriage. She spread it on the ground and patted it smooth. Then she put the lacy square cloth in the middle, patting it smooth too. She moved with precision, tilting her head this way and that, as though judging her work. "Well, don't just stand there," she said, without looking at me. "Help."

"Help prepare a party for your dolls? And give them food they can't even eat? That's worse than spoiled."

Miss Susanna went to the carriage and took out plates and those serviettes. She placed them carefully around the edges of the white cloth. She moved with stiff, quick precision, her chin still high, her shoulders squared. "One for Geraldine. One for Eleanor. One for Alexandra. One for me." There was still one plate and serviette in her hands. Her shoulders seemed to rise a little toward her ears, as if in question.

"Five," I said softly, as I realized. "One . . . extra."

Our eyes locked.

She put the fifth plate and serviette beside hers. "See? I'm nice. Again. So will you sit and act civilized?"

There was food in that carriage. Lots of it. Saliva filled my mouth. I couldn't speak.

"Well?"

My knees wanted to buckle. But I shook my head. I had come with a goal—to protect little Paddy. I mustn't forget it.

"Suit yourself." Miss Susanna placed the dollies in front of their plates—Geraldine, then Eleanor, then Alexandra. Exactly the order she had said their names in.

"I have a dolly," I said.

Miss Susanna looked me up and down. Then she looked around. "Did you hide her somewhere? Bring her out. Let me see."

"She's at home."

"Hmmm. Is she pretty?"

"She's a bone."

"What do you mean?"

"She's a bone. Carved from a goat shin. She used to have a bit of wool wrapped around her." I felt ashamed saying it that way. Granny had made her a dress. But Miss Susanna would never consider that bit of wool a dress anyway.

"Well, that's stupid."

"She has a name, though."

Miss Susanna took a basket from the carriage and put it beside her place at the cover. Then she sat. She folded her legs and folded her hands in her lap and looked up at me. "Well . . . what's her name?"

"Why should I tell you? I bet you don't even remember my name."

"Lorraine." Miss Susanna's eyes went glassy. Was she about to cry?

I was being so mean. I hated being this mean. If I acted better, maybe she would too.

Miss Susanna lifted her chin higher. "What is your dolly's name?"

"Margaret."

"Margaret. Margaret the Bone." She touched her serviette. Then she touched the serviette at the empty place setting. "Are you going to sit or not?"

"I got sick from eating so much last time."

"Whose fault is that?"

Whose fault is that? I rolled the question around inside my head. I didn't like it the first time she said it and I hated it this time. "And I felt guilty."

Miss Susanna's eyes opened wide. "Why?"

"Everyone's hungry. All the time. But for a moment, I wasn't. I had far more than I needed. And I couldn't even share with my little brother."

Miss Susanna shook her head. "You're daft. I already told you. You're all daft, you Irish."

"Don't you say that!"

"You are. You don't need anyone to give you food. I rode with my dad through town. We went all the way to Galways. We stayed there five whole days. I saw lots of poor people. Dirty. In rags. Skinny, like you. I even saw a man run naked in the snow. A chimney sweep he was. But you know what else I saw?"

I wouldn't give her the satisfaction of asking.

"I saw boats get loaded up with cattle to carry away to sell. Cattle and hogs. Big hogs. You know what that means?"

I felt too thick to dare an answer.

"Dad explained to me, but he didn't have to. I could see for myself. It means you could eat, all you Irish could eat, but you don't. You're starving yourselves for no good reason. You're stubborn idiots."

Starvation in the midst of abundance.

That pounding I'd become used to started up in my head again.

"See? You have no answer. You admit it. I bet even you have hogs."

All the hammering in my head made me sway on my feet.

"Eat your hogs, why don't you?"

"We have Muc," I said. "She sleeps with us and keeps us warm. Without her we'd freeze at night."

"Don't you have peat for a fire? That proves how daft you are. There's a peat bog not far from here. Anyone can cut peat from it. We have tons of peat."

"Da goes to that peat bog every other day. Sometimes we help him, Paddy and me. But we can't carry much." I was speaking faster and faster. I had to get it all out. "Da gets shattered from the long walk, especially the walk home, carrying most of that weight—really, nearly all. Then he sells it. Every bit he carries, he sells. We keep only what Paddy and I carry."

"Why don't . . ."

"Shhhh. Please, Miss Susanna. Give a listen. It's important that you understand how hard it is for us. Da says it's barely worth all that work for the peat, because the man he sells it to pays him less these days. Seems everyone's cutting turf from the bogs to sell as fuel in the big city. That Galways you visited.

So there's plenty of fuel for sale—and the price has dropped. That's how it works."

"But why sell it at all? Use it to heat your home."

"Where else would we get money?"

"You have money. From the grains. My dad told me that before winter started, the boats leaving Galways for England were loaded with grains. And that's another thing. You could eat your own grains. No one in England is hungry. It's pure stupid that people in Ireland are."

"We have to sell our grains to pay the rent to the landlord. To your da."

"Rent couldn't cost that much."

"It does. And your da's steward wouldn't bargain at all."

"I don't believe you."

"Da told him we needed some of those grains for food, but he wouldn't listen."

"You're wrong."

"I heard him speaking to Da back in autumn. After the murrain hit."

"What's the murrain?"

"The blight. You know . . . the sickness that ruined our harvest. Your da's steward said, 'What the devil do we care about your black spuds?'"

Miss Susanna kept shaking her head, but slowly now, more and more slowly.

"He said, 'It was not us that turned them black.' He gave Da two days to pay the rent, or we'd get evicted."

Miss Susanna's face was blank. "Evicted?"

"Kicked off the land," I said. "Lose our home."

Miss Susanna stared at me. "Are you sure?"

I nodded. "He said, 'Act nice about it too.' He said, 'Even if you pay up, we can evict you. Just on a whim.' He said—"

"That's enough." Miss Susanna pressed her lips together in a thin line. Then she took a deep breath. "It doesn't matter what he said, that wasn't Dad. That was the steward. I never liked him. He clumps when he walks. And he snorts and spits. I knew he wasn't nice. I only met him in late November, when I came here so that Dad wouldn't have to spend the holidays alone. But I knew instantly that he was awful." She pointed at the empty place. "Sit." She screwed up her mouth. "Please."

I wanted to keep talking. I wanted to ask her if she really thought it was fair that her Englishman da got rent from my Irishman da when this was Irish land. Was it fair that she lived in a castle with who knew what kinds of luxuries when we lived in a one-room cottage with nothing more than shelves and a table and stools? Was it fair that her da rode around in a carriage wherever he wanted doing whatever he wanted while my da and ma toiled every day of the week? Worst of all, was it fair she had food to spare when we were so hungry? Oh, I had so many questions. She'd fight me hard over them, I knew.

But her telling me to sit and then saying "please" so sweetly somehow stole all my gumption. I didn't want to obey her, yet my legs had a mind of their own. They carried me to the cover and then they folded under me. "I won't eat, though," I said.

"How is not eating going to help anyone?"

There had to be an answer. A good one. But my mind was muddled. I shrugged.

Miss Susanna opened the basket and put a plate of meat slices in the center of the white cloth. They had something swirled through them.

I sniffed the air. I remembered that smell, from the old days. Memories of sausages. "Pork."

"The very best. Dad bought a whole side of hog in Galways. This is rolled pork roast. Cook makes it the way I like, with apple and onion stuffing. She's being extra nice to me from now through New Year's, so I won't be missing England too much this holiday. Oh, the Christmas roasts in a fine English carvery. You could never imagine how good they are." Miss Susanna took two forks out of the basket. She put one by my plate. With the other, she speared a piece of meat and put it on her plate. She looked at me, and there was no doubt what she expected me to do.

The inside of my nose hurt, like I was about to cry. If I had held out a minute more, I would have cried. But I didn't. Temptation won; I put a piece of meat on my plate. What a weak mess of a spirit I had.

We ate. Never in my life had I eaten anything so good. It sat on my tongue like a blessing, like the host in the holy mass, like everything good I'd ever hoped for. My nose ran. My eyes blurred. I chewed as slowly as I could. It had to last.

"And I have a treat for you." Miss Susanna reached into the basket and pulled out something. A spud sat in her palm like a brown egg, all full of promise. "Cook's been making them for me, ever since I last saw you. They're really hard to find. Most are rotten. So Cook has to pay a lot for the good ones. I've brought one out here every day since the last time you visited, in the hope that you'd show up again." She put the spud on my plate.

"Did you eat all the others?"

"What a revolting idea!" Miss Susanna wrinkled her nose and gave a quick laugh. "I fed them to the chickens. They seem to like them. They've been laying more eggs ever since I started. So I guess spuds are good for something." She pointed at the spud. "Eat it. Go on."

I ate the spud. The spud that would have otherwise gone to a chicken. Tears ran down my cheeks into my mouth.

"What's the matter? Don't you like it?"

"It's perfect."

"Then don't cry."

"It's so perfect, I have to cry."

"That's daft. Stop it, right now!"

But my eyes kept leaking. "I can't stand it."

"What? What can't you stand?"

"I can't stand it that my belly's full and Paddy's is empty . . . and not just Paddy . . . Deirdre and . . . really, all of them."

"Always the same thing." Miss Susanna wrung her hands. Then she plopped them in her lap in defeat. "I'll try to help. But you can't bring your brother. He might tell. You can't bring any of your friends, either. Just that baby. You can bring that baby next time you come."

"Baby?"

"Baby Nola."

"Baby Nola." My voice broke.

"I've been thinking about her. I want to hold her. I want to feel her skin. You said it was soft. Bring her."

I shook my head. "I can't."

"Don't you get tired of being so stubborn all the time?"

"She's dead."

Miss Susanna's mouth dropped open. Her face went slack. Then her eyes brimmed over with tears. "She got so hungry she died?"

No. She died of the fever that came from the lice that were on the beggars. But it would get too confusing to explain all that to Miss Susanna. And I could see how bad she felt right now. . . . I could see that baby Nola's death might be able to be used to help the rest of them. And that anger I'd felt as I was walking here, that anger that had turned to fury and then disappeared like a phantom, it was back now. So I gave in to temptation a second time; I nodded.

Miss Susanna hugged herself and her face was as sad as faces get.

"That's what made me know I had to come back to your castle," I said. "I had to knock on your door and ask for food, we need it so bad." At least that much was truth.

"You were actually coming to the castle door?" Miss Susanna grabbed my arm. "You can't do that. If Dad knew I spent time with you, we'd both get in trouble. He told me I must never mingle with Irish children. Never ever. It's dangerous."

"Dangerous?"

"You're all a bunch of ruffians."

"I'm not a ruffian."

"No, I suppose you're not. The others are bad and crazy. You're the exception."

I was no exception. I was just like everyone else. I stared at her.

"And you all carry disease."

I had no answer to that. Maybe we did. Maybe those fever lice were on us and we just hadn't gotten sick yet. Maybe I was infecting Miss Susanna even as we sat here in the middle of the trees. Oh, how I hoped not. But all that was beside the point. "Miss Susanna, we need food right away." My mind was racing ahead, as though the pork had joined hands with the fury and together they warmed it, like a peat fire inside my head. "And it should matter to your da. If we all die of hunger, who's going to work the fields come spring? You'll go hungry then too."

"I won't be here in spring."

"Your da will be, won't he?"

"He might. At least part of the time. He travels back and forth to England." Miss Susanna's face filled with alarm. "Let's pray. Dad always says prayers are the right things for girls."

"Ma prays all the time. I haven't seen any difference come from it."

"Well, your ma's Irish. An Irish prayer is worth only a tenth of an English prayer. So if I pray with you, God will surely hear."

"You say the worst things."

"Don't go getting all spiteful again. I didn't mean anything

by it. It's just how things are. You were born Irish. Bad luck."
Miss Susanna wiped her cheeks and frowned. "There won't be
any more deaths anyway. Babies are weak. They die easy. That
baby Nola will be the only one."

"Deirdre and Quinlin and Riley aren't babies. And they're
about to die too." I hoped I was fibbing again. I hoped it so
hard. I should have bitten my tongue to keep it from saying
such awful things, but I couldn't stop now. I blurted out the
worst: "And my little brother . . . Paddy . . . he's skin and bones."

"Like Margaret the Bone."

"Nearly."

"Is that all your friends? Paddy and Deirdre and Quinlin
and Riley? Just the four?"

I shook my head. "There are eighteen of them."

"Eighteen! I don't even know eighteen other children back
home. I sometimes play with two neighbor girls. And, well,
maybe one of them doesn't really like me. But eighteen . . . how
can you remember all their names?"

"Seventeen, now that baby Nola's dead. But eighteen if you
count Paddy. Eighteen children in five families."

"Well, that's too many. Far too many. Families are wonderful, I know that. But you Irish are irresponsible, having children
you can't take care of."

"I think I don't like you." The words had come out on their
own. Here I was hoping to convince her to help, and I was
being mean. But those words were true.

Miss Susanna blinked and blinked. I could see she was trying not to show how much I'd hurt her. "Go home now. Let

that food settle in your stomach. Then see how you feel about me. And when you come back—"

"I won't come back. If you won't help us, there's no reason to come back."

"When you come back, bring Margaret the Bone." Miss Susanna's eyes had narrowed. Her lips were pressed together again. She made me suspicious.

"What are you thinking about?"

"There's no point talking about it till I know more. I'll tell you next time you come. And you'll be happy. Believe me."

I did believe her. Spoiled girls like her could make things happen . . . that's why I'd come here, after all. "I will come, then. But I'm bringing Paddy."

"You can't."

"I will."

"I could get very tired of you, Lorraine."

"Then we won't come. And you'll have no company."

"I have my dolls."

"Sure, and just how good are they at conversation?"

Miss Susanna's face hardened. "Come alone or you'll ruin everything. And you'll be sorry if you do that. Really. So do what I say. Come alone. And come soon. No more dallying like last time. It's Christmas next week Friday. Come before Christmas, for sure."

I squeezed the bridge of my nose and closed my eyes a moment, like Da did when he was thinking something over.

"And come early in the morning. As soon as you wake up." She pursed her lips in determination. "That's important."

Part 3

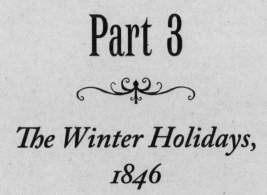

The Winter Holidays, 1846

CHAPTER ELEVEN

Smell

The wide band of kelp along the strandline looked nearly black in the sunshine. The water had deposited it there as it retreated. High tide was hours ago, so despite the cold, this remarkable sun had won; the kelp was dried and almost crisp. We gathered it, we children, and handed it to the adults, who packed it tight and thick into the waiting baskets. I moved without thinking, carrying load after load. The sun toasted my back and neck and arms. It comforted me. And this work comforted me. I wouldn't think. I couldn't think. The sun above and the kelp in my arms and the sand underfoot—that's all there was in the whole world. I breathed deep of the fishy smell. I could do this forever.

"Enough," said Fiona's da, at last. "The baskets are full. This should do it."

The mas and das nodded. They took a basket in each hand. There were still many on the beach, though. I counted: eleven. "We can come back for the other baskets," said Fiona's ma. "Wait for us. Stay together and be wide—use your eyes." And they left, all of them, marching solemnly back along the boreen to the cottiers' huts.

We looked out to sea. The seal sandbar glistened with sleek

bodies. They lay slantwise every which way. The whole colony looked cozy and friendly. It looked like they didn't have a care in the world.

"They're basking," said Teagan. "They love this sun."

"They bask in any weather," said Murray. "I saw them out there last week in a ferocious wind. It has nothing to do with the sun."

"Yeah? I still bet they love the sun. I love it. I wish I could swim out there and bask with them."

"Cut off the ructions. You sound like you're sister and brother, you do. Worse than sister and brother, in fact. Come on." Neil waved them over, from where he knelt with his brothers. "Come help us make this sand wall."

"It's a barrier," said Corey.

"Against the bad ones," said little Aeden.

The bad ones. No one asked who they were. We all simply built sand walls, high and long.

But pretty soon Emmet stood up and walked the length of the wall, kicking it in. "We can't just fooster around doing nothing important till they come back. Come on. Let's carry these baskets home." He picked up a basket and held it to his chest, both skinny arms wrapped around it like rope.

Murray did the same.

Carrick wrapped his arms around a basket. He straightened to full height, then staggered backward and fell. A simple basket of kelp . . . and he fell, he was so weakened. He got to his feet slowly and stood over the basket. Red bloomed up his neck.

Sheelagh came up beside him. She closed a hand around one side of the big arc of the basket handle. Carrick looked around at the rest of us, his cheeks aflame now. No boy was used to being helped by his little sister. But he blinked and clasped the other side of the basket handle.

The rest of us paired up: someone big with someone smaller, a basket between them. Little Paddy and I shared one, of course, though he was more hanging on for support. But that still left two baskets on the sand.

I took one in my free hand.

The others stared. But I had the energy. Why not? The rest seemed frail and unsteady, so it was only right for me to do more work. And it made me feel less guilty.

Emmet fixed his eyes on me. Then he shifted his basket to one hand and picked up the last basket with his other. So now he was carrying two all by himself.

We walked back to the cottiers' huts slowly.

The mas stood back with us while the das arranged the kelp all around the sides and roof of the hut that Deirdre and Quinlin and Riley and baby Nola had lived in. It wasn't a big job. This hut was just sticks and turf, built over a ditch that the das had worked together to dig out large enough for a room. So the sides above that ditch weren't high at all, and the roof was just a mishmash of sod. All in that family were dead now, all but the da. No one else among us had taken the fever, though. The other cottier mas had scrubbed the insides of all four huts, soaking them with salt water. But my ma said that treatment wasn't enough for the hut that had held the fever. Salt water was good, but it just wasn't enough.

That's why we'd gathered the kelp. The fever hut was too damp now to catch fire easily. The dried kelp would make the difference.

Little Paddy nestled against Ma's side as the flames licked gentle at first, but when those flames suddenly flared, his body convulsed and he grabbed her tight. I put my hand on his shoulder from behind. The whole hut was engulfed now. Black smoke looped high and ugly against the clear blue sky. The heat came strong and hard as a wall. It hurt. We stepped back fast. The noise was loud, cracking and crashing. It nearly deafened me. If I'd screamed, no one could have heard.

I looked over at the da who had lived in that hut. The da of Deirdre and Quinlin and Riley and baby Nola. He sat on the ground like a broken thing and stared at the flames. His face was black from the smoke, with red streaks where the tears rolled down. Da and Fiona's da pulled him farther back. The broken da didn't care about the heat. He didn't even seem to notice it.

Alana was at my side, shaking her head.

"Where will he live now?" I pointed with my eyes at the broken da.

"The workhouse in Clifden."

I sucked in a gasp. "No." Everyone knew the workhouse was a horrible place.

"Don't get upset," said Kearney. "They probably won't take him anyway. They turn away the sick."

"But he's not sick," Alana said.

"What do you mean?" said Emmet. "Then why won't any of us take him in?"

He was right. Ma would never let our family take him in, I would bet anything on that. No one could be sure that broken da wasn't harboring the fever.

But none of us said that.

Alana pressed her knuckles against her chin. "The workhouse will take him, I just know it. They're supposed to take people who have nowhere to go."

And if the workhouse did take him in, and if he did harbor the black fever, what would happen to everyone else in the workhouse?

There was silence for a moment. I could almost breathe our fear.

We had to be wrong. That da mustn't have the fever. *Please.*

"Lucky him," said Emmet at last. He sneered. "He'll die of the cold even before they get a chance to work him to death."

"But he'll be inside," I said. "It can't be that cold inside."

"You know nothing." Emmet poked me in the shoulder. "Nothing."

I opened my mouth to protest, but the look on Emmet's face silenced me. It seemed like pure hatred. He turned his back and walked off into the dark. I looked at Alana. "What did I do?"

"Nothing," said Alana.

"He's talking about the blankets," said Kearney.

"What?"

"The workhouse ran out of blankets long ago. That poor da

won't have any bedding." Alana took Kearney by the hand and they walked off after Emmet.

How would that broken da stay warm without blankets?

Who would he tell stories to at night?

Who would he hold and kiss?

I walked over to Ma's other side, buried my head under her arm, and sobbed.

When the flames died, Fiona's ma spoke loud. "Don't go near for at least a day. It'll smolder for a while. You could get burned. You hear me." She was still looking at the remains of the hut, but we knew she was talking to us kids. She needn't have wasted her efforts, though—none of us was moving forward. I couldn't imagine we'd ever want to touch the charred remains of that home.

Deirdre and Quinlin and Riley and baby Nola.

And their ma. I mustn't forget their ma.

They were buried out back, without even a stone to mark the spot. Five bodies in a hole, no coffins. The other das had dug the hole, but the broken da was the only one to carry the bodies and lay them in it. He was the only one who dared touch them, after all.

Not marking a grave with a pile of stones was unheard of, but this grave was a secret. Ma had told me. I didn't know whether the other kids knew or not. She made me swear not to tell. The landlord never would have allowed their burial here. But the only other choice was awful; they'd have been thrown in the new mass graveyard behind the workhouse in town. The workhouse where the broken da would now go to live.

I didn't really care where they were buried. What mattered, what hurt, was that they were no more.

And suddenly I wondered how many fields had unmarked graves. Secrets. My throat felt raw, as though I'd been screaming hard and long.

Alana's ma stood nearby. She shook her head at Ma. "There will be no candle in the window tonight. Not in any of our huts. Mary and Joseph can find better places to welcome them, and that's the truth."

So it was Christmas Eve. I'd actually lost track.

"That's the truth, indeed," said Ma. "I'll see you at the midnight mass."

Alana's ma gave a small smile. "There will be a fiddler with dancing in the streets, no matter the cold. And Francis can play the bones. Oh, how I love listening to him clacking away."

"And who's got the strength to dance?" said Ma. "But maybe just trying will do us all good. Just acting like there's something to dance about can heal the spirit. You and your husband, you've always been grand dancers."

"I won't be there. Not me." It was Alana's da. He was walking past slowly, and he didn't stop. "Not after this. This is too much. No dancing. And no mass. Mass is not for me. Ever again."

Alana's ma opened her mouth. Then closed it. She walked over to Kearney and Kyla and led them each by the hand into their hut.

Ma took little Paddy by one hand and me by the other, just like Alana's ma had done with her children. She squeezed our hands and gave a little sigh. Then we walked toward our cottage.

Deirdre and Quinlin and Riley and baby Nola. And their ma. Every step was a name inside my head. Every step shot pain all through me.

I pulled on Ma's hand. "Why are you going to mass tonight?"

"What on earth can you mean?"

"Alana's da said—"

"Don't go making trouble, Lorraine. What Alana's da says has nothing to do with you."

"Alana said the workhouse has no blankets, so that broken da's going to die of the cold."

"Broken da—you're right, he's broken. But the workhouse has blankets. They must."

"My question is real, Ma. Why would you go to mass tonight?"

"It's the celebration of the birth of God's son, who is God himself. You know that."

"After what God just did . . ."

"Hush, Lorraine."

"But why would He let—"

"Hush. God is being God. That's all there is to it. If you don't understand it, you'd best just hush."

That's what Da said to Ma after baby Nola died. *Hush.* We all had to hush. We all had to keep the faith. I didn't see why. When I was little, I had talked with God all the time. Anything bothered me, I jabbered to God about it. And I always felt better afterward. Because I knew God had heard me and understood me. He knew how hard it was to be me. He knew everything, everyone, and He cared about us all. That alone comforted me—being listened to like that.

Only He hadn't listened to Deirdre's prayers. I was sure she'd prayed to Him—because I had, so she must have. All of us had, I was sure. And I was sure Quinlin and Riley had prayed and prayed. And their ma—she must have shuffled around their hut floor on her knees in prayer for days. She must have worn the flesh away to the bone. God hadn't heard her. He hadn't heard any of them.

Or worse, He'd heard and He just didn't care.

My mouth filled with blood. I must have bitten my tongue. I swallowed and went back to reciting names inside my head. Deirdre and Quinlin and Riley and baby Nola and their ma. Reciting names was so much better than thinking. Deirdre and Quinlin and Riley and baby Nola.

We walked the rest of the way to our cottage in silence. Da arrived soon after. I didn't know where he'd been. Ma hugged him, then served the gruel early. And little Paddy and I went to our sleeping mat.

Little Paddy nestled against me now, like he'd nestled against Ma watching the flames. I put my arm around him. His hair tickled my nose. It smelled of smoke. His whole body smelled of smoke. Mine probably did too. I wondered how long the smell would cling to us.

Da began his telling. He'd gotten into tellings again for the past week, ever since baby Nola had died. Who knew why, but I was glad of it. I'd missed his tellings more than anything.

He surprised me, though. I'd expected the tale of the wren.

More than a thousand years before, in the time when the Vikings were invading Ireland, a bold wren did a bad thing. Good Irish soldiers had been waiting in hiding, to fight off the Vikings as they got off their ships. But a wicked wren, sent by the devil himself, beat his wings on the soldiers' shields. He drummed so loud, the Vikings were warned. What a wretched betrayal. I was fascinated by the wickedness of that wren. He sang so sweet, then look what he did! That *sleveen*—that rogue and trickster. Da told this tale all through the holiday, every year, and he always started on Christmas Eve.

But tonight Da didn't do that. He told the tale of the birth of Jesus. Ma must have whispered to him what I said about not going to mass. I wasn't sad, though. I liked this tale too. I had just really wanted the tale of the wren tonight. I had wanted someone to be angry at—someone to blame. Someone easy . . . like a thick and treacherous bird.

Nothing was easy, though. Not anymore.

I stroked little Paddy's hair as Da talked on and on. I could tell from the sound of Paddy's breath that he was asleep. I shut my eyes and let Da's words rock me, back and forth, till I finally drifted to sleep.

In my dream, baby Nola was in my arms, crying. Why was she in my arms? Where was Deirdre? This was Deirdre's responsibility, not mine. But the baby cried and no one else was around to console her. I needed to get inside someplace and rock her to sleep. I knocked on doors. I banged on them. Not a one would open. No windows showed lights. I ran with the babe in my arms along the streets of town, and we passed no one. No one at all.

We ran along the tiny boreens now, from cottage to cottage. No one passed. No one but birds. Squawking birds, flapping their wings so loud. And Nola was crying loud. Shrieking, really. How could such a little baby make such a loud noise? Louder than the crack and crash of fire. It was so loud, I couldn't think. I ran like someone gone in the head, as fast as I could, not knowing where, just away, away. And I tripped. Baby Nola flew out of my arms, smack on the ground. Silent.

Dead.

My fault.

I woke in a panic. Sweat had soaked my nightshift. I panted into the black air. My heart was like that wren, drumming so loud it would betray me and everyone else would wake. I waited, ready to apologize. But no one else woke. Gradually my heart stopped pounding.

I wiped the snot from my nose. Some things were my fault, true. But not everything.

Not everything.

I listened. I could hear Muc and little Paddy breathing. But that was all. Ma and Da must still be at midnight mass. It was Christmas morn by now.

I whispered to them all—it didn't matter that they weren't listening or weren't even in the room to hear—I whispered, "*Nollaig shona daoibh*—Happy Christmas to all."

The words felt strange. Happy? Would we ever be happy again?

I put my hands to my face and smelled the burned wood of the fever hut.

CHAPTER TWELVE

Saints

Christmas Day was nothing but rain—cold, hard, driving rain. Despite that, I expected Ma to insist we tramp all the way into town. After all, she and Da had attended mass in the night but little Paddy and I hadn't. It wasn't a sin not to receive Communion on Christmas—not like on Easter. But still, not going on this special day would have been a first. Ma stood by the hearth, her arms crossed at her chest, and I knew she was trying to figure out what to do.

Little Paddy coughed. Then he coughed and coughed and coughed. I didn't know if he was faking it, and I bet Ma didn't either—after all, who wanted to go stand outside at a mass in this wet chill? But even if she doubted him, she rushed to him and carried him to the stool and sat stroking him on her lap.

The door opened and the wind swept water in. We all stared. Muc scrambled to her feet and let out a snort. The man who stood hunched forward in the doorway held a brace of hares in one hand and a small hide bag in the other. He tossed the bag a little ways into the room and used his free hand to lift the visor of his flat cap and give us a peek at his wet grin.

"Odran!" Ma slapped a hand to her cheek in shocked delight. "Odran!"

"Think you're a silver herring, do you? Without the sense to get out of the rain?" Da smiled and came forward. "Come on in, *dearthái mór*—big brother."

Uncle Odran had to stoop to clear the low doorway as he sloshed into the room; he was even bigger than Da. Da secured the door behind him, then they clasped each other tight, despite Uncle Odran's wet jumper.

Uncle Odran handed his cap to Da, set the hares on the floor, then stripped off his jumper. It was big and thick and I recognized the pattern: Those diamond stitches ensured success, and the twisting ones mimicked paths along cliffs. I was sure Granny had made it for him. Years and years ago probably. Maybe even before I was born. Da hung it over a hook on the wall, and I watched the water run off it and pool on the hard ground floor. His shirt underneath wasn't even wet. Now Uncle Odran turned in a slow circle, looking around the room. He made a full revolution before he stopped and his eyes took me in.

But I stepped backward toward the wall. After all, I hadn't seen him for more than a year. I felt thick and shy.

Uncle Odran gave me a close-lipped smile and nodded, as though he understood. "Good to see you, Lorraine."

I nodded back.

He picked up the hares, went over to Ma's stool, bent, and kissed her on the cheek. Then he got down on one knee. "And you, Paddy. Last I saw of you, you were barely worth mentioning. Now look what a grand fellow you are."

It wasn't true. Little Paddy's glassy eyes were sunk so deep in his head, I had the urge to go snatch him from Ma's arms and cradle him in my own. Why hadn't I noticed before what was happening to his eyes? I imagined what Uncle Odran must be thinking, how disturbed he must be to see his nephew with less flesh than a crow and hardly any bigger.

"Do you know who I am?" Uncle Odran's voice was gentler now.

"Are those hares for us?"

Uncle Odran held the brace high and seemed to consider it. "You mean these two hares?"

"I do. Are they for us?"

"They are."

"They're dead," said little Paddy.

"You noticed. That's what makes them good to eat. Have you ever eaten hare before?"

I tensed up. *Oh, please, don't let him ask me.*

"I have not," said little Paddy.

"Good. That makes them a special gift. A delicious gift."

"Are you Saint Nicholas, then?"

Uncle Odran laughed. "I guess I could be. For a day or two, at least."

"Don't tease," said Ma. "This is your Uncle Odran, Paddy. Remember? He's Da's *dearthálr mór*. And I sure hope he'll stay more than a day or two."

"Not so quick." Uncle Odran held up a finger. "I've got something in that bag over there." He jerked his chin toward the leather bag, which Muc was pushing around in the corner with her snout. "Would you fetch it for me, Lorraine? Would you do that, darling?"

I yanked the bag away from Muc, who looked at me accusingly, and I carried it over to Uncle Odran, then quickly stepped away again.

"Thank you." Uncle Odran still held the hares high, but he reached inside his bag with his other hand and pulled out a ball the color of the setting sun.

"What is that thing?" said Ma.

"They call it an orange. It's a fruit. From Spain."

"A fruit in winter?"

"Exactly."

Ma blinked. Da leaned in for a look. Even I came closer.

Uncle Odran held the orange under little Paddy's nose. "What do you think of that smell?"

Little Paddy sniffed. "It's good."

"The best. Everyone should smell it." He handed it to Da.

Da smelled it. "*Maith*—good." He passed it to Ma.

Ma smelled it. "*Maith.*" She held it out to me.

I took it in both hands and pressed it to my nose. The smell was as sweet as the perfume of flowers. I didn't want to give it up.

"So now, Paddy, my boy, this orange is yours." Uncle Odran nodded at me.

Reluctantly, I placed the fruit in little Paddy's hands.

"*Maith,*" said little Paddy.

"And I have one for your ma and another for your da and a fourth for your beautiful sister." He looked at me and I realized he knew how I felt about that orange. My cheeks heated. He turned back to little Paddy. "I guess that means I really am Saint Nicholas."

"Da said Saint Nicholas couldn't come this year. He said we'd celebrate with playing games instead of having gifts."

"Your da makes a lot of mistakes. Always has."

Ma shook her head, but she smiled and reached out for the brace of hares. "Here, Odran, you hold your nephew while Lorraine and I get these hares cleaned. And I'm not about to ask you where you hunted them."

"Rest assured I won't answer," said Uncle Odran. "Strategic amnesia strikes again."

Ma laughed. "No, I won't ask. A violation like that could land you where no one wants to go."

So Ma and I skinned hares and made a stew of them with cabbage, while little Paddy sat mesmerized on Uncle Odran's lap, turning that orange over and over in his hands, and Da and his brother talked softly. Mostly about Granny and her passing and how Uncle Odran hadn't received Da's letter. Lots of letters wound up in the Dead Letter Office. Everyone who went home after a long stay away expected to learn of major changes in their absence—and death was getting to be more common among those changes.

Then Da and Uncle Odran moved closer together and talked even softer. I had trouble catching more than just snatches because of the noise of the fire that Da had set to crackling, so I finally stopped trying. What did it matter anyway? The important thing was that so long as they were talking, any thought of tramping through the rain all that long way to mass in town was banished.

When there was nothing left to do but stir, I washed the

hare skins and set them way off to the side to dry slowly. The fur was dense and soft. I rubbed my cheek against it.

"You thinking of making yourself something from those hides, Lorraine?" Ma studied me.

I'd have loved to. I couldn't remember ever touching anything so luxurious. But what? That itself was a giant problem, I realized. I shook my head. "They're not big enough for me." I smoothed them with both hands. One was yellowish. One was brown. They were beautiful. I swallowed. "But they'd make Paddy a grand vest."

"True. That's what he needs." Ma turned back to stirring the stew.

So as simple as that, the grandest gift I might have ever gotten went to little Paddy instead. But it's what I deserved after how wicked I'd been. I had a lot more sacrifices ahead if I was ever going to atone.

The room slowly filled with the way too rare smell of meat, a hearty, dark smell that made me woozy. Finally, we ate, and a proper midday meal for Christmas it was, indeed.

Little Paddy chewed thoughtfully on the meat, but in the end he ate barely anything. Still, barely anything was better than nothing. He went over to our sleeping mat and stretched out. He'd been napping in the afternoon more and more often these days, like he used to do when he was little.

"He didn't enjoy the hare," said Uncle Odran.

"He probably did," said Ma. "But he's not used to having anything rich to eat. None of us are."

"Lorraine's enjoying it," said Uncle Odran, looking me in the face.

I stopped moving mid-chew. *Please, please don't let him ask me if this was my first time eating hare.*

He smiled, and again I felt like he was looking inside my head. "Lots more than Paddy."

He was right. I was eating too much. More than I should for my size. I didn't know why I was being so greedy. The others needed this food much more than I did. I pushed my bowl away.

"Don't stop," said Uncle Odran. "It's good that you're eating. It'll keep you strong and healthy."

"It's well you're looking, Odran," said Da with surprise in his voice.

"The food in the Liverpool prison was better than the food in the workhouse in Dublin. Far better."

Ma looked quick from Uncle Odran to me.

Prison? My throat went tight. But I stayed polite; I asked, "What's Liverpool?"

"A town in England. I was living in the workhouse in Dublin for a year. You know where Dublin is, don't you?"

"I do. It's a grand city."

"A grand city full of walking skeletons. Anyway, I was working there, cutting stone for ten hours a day, till the public works program started in the autumn and put me out in the countryside building roads. Then the rains came in November, hard and cold. You know how it's been lately. People were so emaciated they were dropping right there on the job."

"Dropping?" I asked.

Uncle Odran closed his eyes a moment. "All that for nine

pennies a day," he said at last. "That's when I got involved with political action."

"What's that mean?"

Uncle Odran looked at Da.

Da lifted both eyebrows. "Go ahead."

"But, Francis . . . ," said Ma.

"She's a cunning girl, Catherine. She's working like the rest of us, and suffering like the rest of us. She has a right to know things. Besides, after the past week, she's had to grow up. All the kids have."

Uncle Odran pushed my bowl of stew back toward me. "Eat. So long as you're eating, I'll talk."

I put a spoonful of stew in my mouth and chewed slowly.

"People are getting together, you know. Trying to take care of each other. It's not right that all the food Ireland produces goes to make the English fat while the Irish starve. There are good people out there who say it's enough now. Too much. Ireland belongs to the Irish."

"Except it doesn't," said Ma. "Nothing belongs to us."

"By any measurement of justice, it should. They stole it."

"Tell me," I blurted out. "Tell me all about it."

"It's a long story," said Ma. "Things that go back centuries and centuries. It doesn't matter now."

"Of course it does," said Uncle Odran. "And the girl should know—shouldn't you, Lorraine? We don't have to start at the beginning. We can start with the 1600s—with how the English settlers formed so many new boroughs on Irish land, they managed to take over our parliament. Then in 1649 the devil himself came—Oliver Cromwell. The king of England sent Devil Cromwell here to tame the wild Irish."

"Were we wild?" I asked.

"We've never been tame," said Da softly.

"But we weren't lawless like Cromwell." Uncle Odran scratched his cheek. "That devil had an army whose solution to any problem was slaughter."

"You mean guns?"

"Guns and guns and guns. Then Devil Cromwell wound up short of funds to pay his soldiers. So he gave them Irish land in payment. Farm land." Uncle Odran crossed his arms on the table and leaned toward me. "Our farm land."

"But how could that happen? Who could think that was fair?"

"We were Catholic," said Da. "They weren't. That made them think they were better than us. They felt they deserved the land."

Ma shook her head. "Enough already. The land has been theirs for two hundred years. It doesn't belong to us anymore. It never will again. It takes money to buy land."

"Oh, Catherine," said Uncle Odran, "if you could only hear John Mitchel speak. And Thomas Francis Meagher, what a grand man he is—decent and wise."

"Meagher's gone too far," said Da. "When he was talking peaceful action, his words were repeated by everyone. They came all the way to Clifden. He gave us hope. But from the last I've heard, he's changed."

"Because they don't listen, the English. Meagher is right:

Sometimes justice calls for a drop of blood, and sometimes, many thousands of drops of blood."

Ma instantly stiffened. "Did you do something wrong, Odran?" Her voice was screechy. "Did you take up arms? Is that how you wound up in prison?"

"I'm not a saint, Catherine. And I don't promise to become one. But all I did this autumn was talk. That's all, I swear. I spread the word so that people would come to meetings and get organized. I finished my day of hard labor and then dragged myself through the streets, stopping anyone I passed." He shrugged. "And then I got the idea of going to Liverpool. Lots of Irish have emigrated there—there and Glasgow—but I chose Liverpool because it was closer, cheaper to get to. I figured I'd find a job easy and a community to live in and tell English people the truth about what was happening in Ireland. If I did that, I could make a real difference. The Englishmen who listened could prevent the misery from becoming a true slaughter—a slaughter worse than in Devil Cromwell's time."

Uncle Odran shook his head and gave a lopsided and rueful smile. "I failed right off—no one would hire me. By then the Irish immigrants in Liverpool were living in such overcrowded quarters that there were fever outbreaks, so everyone was afraid of us. At the first sound of my Irish accent, people turned away, no matter how much I pleaded. I was starving in Liverpool, even worse than in Dublin." He lifted an eyebrow. "You know that couldn't last. One morning I snatched a pasty from a baker's cart and landed in prison. And you know what? For the first time in a year and a half, I ate my fill. More than in Clifden,

more than in Dublin, more than on the streets of Liverpool."
Uncle Odran pinched his own cheek. "Which is why I have
some fat in this here cheek. Plentiful, regular prison food. But
last week someone decided it was more expensive to keep an
Irishman in prison than to send him back home to starve. And
if they let us go right then, it would look like an act of charity,
sending us home for the holiday. So they put all the Irish prisoners on a ship to Dublin. And not just prisoners. They picked
up anyone homeless. Anyone who looked sick. Anyone Irish
they could put their hands on. Those ships carried a motley lot,
they did."

He got up and went to his hide bag and distributed the
three oranges inside it to Ma and Da and me. "English sailors
eat these to keep from getting sick as they travel the seas."

"And they gave you some?" I asked.

"When's the last time an Englishman ever gave you anything?" Uncle Odran looked at me hard.

I thought of Miss Susanna. Could Uncle Odran see the
guilt in my eyes? I looked down.

"Stealing is wrong," said Ma. "You know the saying: Better
is the trouble that follows death than the trouble that follows
shame."

"I disagree. Letting yourself be killed is worse," said Uncle
Odran.

I looked over at little Paddy, asleep on our mat. Letting
everyone you loved be killed was the worst of all. My mouth
went dry.

I turned again to Uncle Odran. "What happened then?"

"When I got off the boat, I met a priest who hadn't gone to bed for five nights. He hadn't taken off his surplice because there was always someone dead, someone who needed Extreme Unction. And he wouldn't let himself stop moving." He made a little snorty noise. "In the month I'd been gone, so many people had come into Dublin from the countryside, already sick and starving, that the workhouses and hospitals and prisons were overcrowded. In six months the cemeteries will be too." He rubbed his mouth with the back of his hand. "So I decided the English were right. Purely by accident, they were right: Going home for the holiday made sense. And you're my home now, because you're the only family I have."

"You can stay as long as you like," said Da.

Ma nodded in agreement.

"I know that. And I thank you. But I only came to tell you I love you."

"*Is eol duit méid mo ghrá duit*—you know how I love you," said Da.

"It's right that we say it to each other," said Uncle Odran. "Each time is maybe the last time. I'm going back to Dublin. You should come too."

"That doesn't make sense," said Ma. "Dublin's a shambles, you said it yourself. Besides, only one person from a household can be on the public works project at once. I know—we have it here, too. What if they said we were one household, seeing as you'd be brothers living together?"

"I'm not going for paid work. I'm going for action. As I see it, we Irish have only two choices if we want to live. Sell what little we have and take a ship west—no one wants us there, but at least we have a better chance than we do going east. Or stand and fight. And that's the truth. I sure won't give up this land to those thieves. You shouldn't either."

Stand and fight. My breath came hard. I had to find a way to stand and fight.

"We have children, Odran," said Ma. "We have Lorraine and Paddy."

"And those children are the most important reason why we have to do this." Uncle Odran looked hard at Da. "There's no farmwork from Christmas Day to Saint Paddy's Day. Catherine can look after the kids. Come with me, Francis."

"Look around you, Odran. What you see is all we have. Nothing in storage. If it weren't for keeping after the cabbage and kale and . . ."

"Catherine and the children can keep after the kitchen garden."

". . . walking hours every other day to cut peat from the bog to sell in town for a few pennies, we'd all starve. Truly."

"And that's not the only reason," said Ma. "Francis shouldn't go—and you shouldn't go either. Fighting—will you listen to yourself? I will never believe that fighting is the right way."

"Then maybe you don't deserve this land," said Uncle Odran.

"I'm as much a child of Ireland as you are, Odran!"

"Then take care of your heritage. Do it as if there was fire in your skin. Do it the Irish way."

"There isn't just one Irish way. You're gone in the head! There's no forcing the sea."

"Spoken like the already drowned."

"Stop it," said Da. He got up from the table and walked back and forth in front of the hearth. "We're family. Nothing can change that." He looked at Ma.

She pressed her lips in a thin line. But she nodded.

"Do you still have your bones?" said Da to Uncle Odran.

Uncle Odran had risen to his feet during the fight. Now he smiled and dropped back down. He reached into his hide bag.

And they played those bones, clacking away all afternoon, while Ma sang.

Part 4

A Cold Start to 1847

CHAPTER THIRTEEN

Plans

It was black in the cottage, like on the night between Christmas Eve and Christmas morn. And I was sitting up again, awakened by a nightmare again. Da rolled from his back to his side to his back to the other side. He moaned in his sleep. Ma let out thin cries now and then. Only little Paddy slept soundly. That's how it had been ever since we'd burned the fever hut. That was two weeks ago. Sleep was just an invitation to fear. And it had gotten worse since the day after New Year's, when Uncle Odran had left. No one wanted him to return to Dublin. It felt like he was going off to sure doom.

He said he hoped he wasn't leaving behind sure doom. And he gave Da his shoes, saying they might help fend off the devils. Thick-soled shoes.

I had the awful feeling that nightmares would be the rule in our cottage for a long time to come. But I'd had enough of them. It was time to stand and fight.

I had no idea what the hour was, but I didn't see any point in staying on this sleeping mat wondering. Besides, I had decided to go meet Miss Susanna again, and I was eager to do it—just climb that hill and tramp on over to her little wooded hiding place—and confront her. Because that's what I was going to do. Uncle Odran had gone all the way to England and tried to make the people there listen to him—he'd tried and failed. But I wouldn't fail. Miss Susanna was lonely, and even bickering with your enemy is less painful than loneliness. Granny had said that. So Miss Susanna would listen. She'd asked me twice, "Whose fault was that?" Now I had the answer. That would be the start. I was cunning, like Da said. I'd convince her.

Miss Susanna had said to come early, when I first woke up. When did she wake up?

But even if she woke late, it didn't matter, because it would take me so long to get there.

I opened the door just the smallest amount and slipped outside. The wind stole my breath. I was so thick! An idiot, like Miss Susanna had said. I should have put on my old jumper. It was too late now. I didn't want to risk waking Ma and Da.

And she'd told me to bring my doll, Margaret. I'd forgotten that, too. My head was empty.

Bo Bo lumbered over toward me. I looked around at the dreary but undeniable dawn. By the time I got back from seeing Miss Susanna, it could be nearly midday, and Bo Bo would be in pain. I'd milk her now, then.

Only the milking bucket was inside too.

There was no choice.

I went back inside.

Ma was sitting up on her sleeping mat. "Lorraine?" she whispered. "What are doing, up and about at this hour?"

It was cold inside, but still so much warmer than outside. I didn't want to go out again. But Miss Susanna would be waiting. "I need the bucket to milk Bo Bo."

"That cow's asleep."

"She's not." I crossed the room and grabbed the bucket. Then I went to the big basket in the corner and dug around till I found my old jumper.

"That's too small for you," said Ma. "I need to make you a new one."

"It serves me fine."

"It does not, and anyone can see that. I'll find the wool somehow. I promise."

"It's warm, Ma. It's a good jumper. Go back to sleep."

She nestled in beside Da again. "You're so good, Lorraine," she mumbled. "I don't know what I'd do without you."

If she knew about my visits to Miss Susanna, she wouldn't say that. Ma was good, and I wasn't good at all. Like Uncle Odran, I was no saint.

But I wanted to be better. I would try. I would try today.

I quick searched for Margaret. I couldn't find her in the usual spots. Maybe she was on the other side of little Paddy. But if I kept feeling around, I might wake him. I slipped outside again without her. The wind cut at my eyes. Thank heavens for the jumper.

I milked Bo Bo. But I wouldn't carry the bucket inside. Ma might not yet be fully back to sleep. So I set it to the side of the door and headed off through the field.

Dawn grew brighter, and I had been wrong before; it didn't seem dreary now at all. The sky was clear and the world smelled clean. A bird flew directly over my head toward the coast. The bill was the color of oranges. For an instant, my mouth filled with the heavenly taste of the fruits Uncle Odran had brought us. That bill told me the bird was a white-fronted goose. There were flocks of them along the coast all autumn and winter. I wondered how this one had managed to get separated from the others. Goofy thing. I hoped it found its goose mates soon.

I walked fast, despite the fact that my feet hurt so bad from the frost on the ground. My determination felt like a fire inside me. Not just in my skin, like Uncle Odran had said, but deep and everywhere. It was as though I could feel my blood pumping through my arms and legs and head and chest like an animal with its own life, its own energy.

Squeak!

What was that? I stopped short.

Up ahead a hare jumped around as though it was insane. It rolled and then righted itself. Its legs shot out spasmodically. Oh! Now I could make out a creature clinging to its back. I hadn't seen it at first because its fur was nearly the same gray brown as the hare's. It was a weasel—the black tip on its tail was unmistakable. It was maybe half the size of the hare, maybe even less. But its mouth was clamped down firmly on the back of the hare's neck and it was going to kill that hare for sure.

I looked around for a rock. The only one I saw was big. It took two hands to lift. I walked closer and hurled it down as hard as I could, aiming for it to land right beside them, to scare that weasel off. But they were still thrashing around wildly, and it hit them.

They stopped moving. I took another step closer. Neither moved. *Please no.* I looked around and found a stick. I poked them. The weasel fell away from the hare. They were both dead.

I hadn't meant to kill either one. All I had wanted was to stop the weasel.

But there they were.

Flesh and bone—meat. Wasting meat was nothing short of a sin these days. When Ma cooked them, this would be the third time I'd eaten hare. Something felt good about that. Soothing. Anyone knew three was a holy number.

I picked up the hare by the ears with one hand and the weasel by the tail with the other, and I marched on over the crest of the hill and down the other side. A drizzle started. Thank heavens again and again for my jumper. The smell of sheep lanolin from the wet wool was already growing stronger. I marched all the way to the stand of trees that I now thought of as the feasting table.

Miss Susanna was leaning against a tree, hugging herself, but when she saw me, she jumped to attention. "It's been three weeks since you last came. Three weeks this time!"

"And Happy Christmas to you too."

"I've come every day. Including Christmas. Including New Year's." She folded her arms across her chest. "I always come early—like I told you to do. What took you so long?"

"You live right over there in the castle. I live far away."

"You should have gotten up earlier."

I almost told her I had to milk Bo Bo before I could leave.

But I remembered how she had talked about cattle and hogs the last time we were together. She wouldn't understand why we didn't kill Bo Bo and eat her. She didn't know anything. If we ate Bo Bo, then where would we get milk? Without buttermilk, what would happen to little Paddy? It was practically the only thing he ate these days. "I got up before dawn."

"Then you should have walked faster." She jerked her chin toward one of my hands, then the other. "What are you doing with a hare and a stoat?"

"A stoat?" I held one hand high and examined the creature that dangled by its tail. "This is a weasel."

"No it's not. Weasels don't have a black tip on their tail."

"What do you know?"

"Weasels live all over England. So do stoats. I've seen them my whole life."

"It doesn't matter what it's called, does it? It's dead."

"Did you kill it? And the hare, too?"

What if I did? I had no right to kill on this land. And I'd never gone hunting anywhere ever—never wanted to. I shrugged.

"Well, put them down. Right now." She turned and went behind a tree. She came back with two round baskets that bulged in the middle and then went straight up. I knew that kind of basket; it was for eggs. One was new and the other was old and battered. Miss Susanna held the old one out toward me.

I walked forward, still clutching my hare and my whatever-it-was, and looked into the basket. "Empty," I said, feeling confused.

"Take it, you idiot. And put down those dead animals. Do what I say."

"I didn't come here to do what you say. I came to talk to you."

She blinked. "I like talking to you, too."

"I don't mean chatting. I came to—"

"We can talk later. I have a plan. And it won't work if we wait much longer because I'm going into town with Dad today. It's all arranged. And, oh, on second thought, I can use that." She held out her hand. "Give me that stoat."

"What? Surely you won't eat him. Not with half a hog in your larder." I clutched his tail tighter. "Besides, he's just one tight little muscle. All the rest of him is hair and skin and bones and claws and teeth. He couldn't satisfy your family."

She wrinkled her nose. "I don't intend to have Cook roast him. Dad wouldn't eat such a thing. Neither would I. I just need to have him, to say I killed him."

"But you didn't kill him."

She shook her head as though she was annoyed. "How did you kill him, anyway?"

"I didn't say I killed him."

"How? Tell me."

I shrugged. "There are rocks everywhere."

"Yes, that works." Miss Susanna wrinkled her nose again, then she yanked hard and grabbed that creature away before I could stop her.

I let out a little yelp. Her family wouldn't eat that stoat, but mine surely would have.

She held the stoat with a straight arm, as far out from her body as it could get. "Don't worry, this stoat will be a good excuse. Put down that hare and follow me, quiet. Absolutely quiet." She walked off with the new basket over her arm and the stoat swinging by its tail from her other arm, out of the woods, but not directly toward the castle. She was making a wide arc around the castle, following a high stone wall that had been knocked down here and there through years of storms.

I stood and watched and felt all my hope evaporating. Miss Susanna might truly be gone in the head. But nothing good would happen if I didn't convince her to help. And not just in some small way; she had to help all of us. So I perched the dead hare in the crook of a tree and grabbed the old basket and ran as fast as I could to catch up with her.

She was nearly to a wide gap in the wall when I finally reached her side. She glanced quick at me and gave a little humph. "So, see that?"

I looked. There was a wooden hut on the side of the wall toward the castle. I nodded.

"You know a henhouse when you see one?"

"Is that a henhouse?" It was larger than any coop I'd ever seen.

"It is indeed. Don't you know anything?" She put the dead stoat on the ground and wiped her hand in the wet grasses. "You can come in and look around, but only for a second."

I followed her through the gap and then into the henhouse. The roof was so tall, even Da could have stood inside. The rancid smell of feathers and old straw was familiar and brought back the memory of mite bites. Both my arms suddenly felt itchy. The roosting bars were staggered like stairs. I'd never seen that arrangement before. In our old coop, there'd been just two roosting bars, one along one side of the coop and one along the other. But, then, we'd had only three hens. These bars were covered with . . . how many? Ten hens—ten! Side by side, in rows, all fluffed up and snuggly. Their feet were hidden under their fat bodies and they slept. I used to love watching the hens sleep, particularly in spring, when Ma would leave the eggs to hatch and there would be little peepers poking out a head or foot from under all that fluff. But I loved more watching them chase one another around in the grasses and dirt.

"It's late morning. They should be outside scratching around," I said.

"They already went outside. They get up early. Not like you. Besides, it's raining."

"Barely," I said.

"Probably it's going to get worse. They sense that, so they came inside. A few of them are still outside." She looked across the hens. "Two in fact—but these ones inside are cunning."

"That's not true. Hens are thick."

"Well, these are cunning for hens."

Cackling came from behind us. I turned and saw a group of nesting boxes in the corner. A hen strutted around an egg. "Fresh laid," I said with a smile. "Look at that proud ma."

"You're lucky." Miss Susanna scooped up the egg and put it in my basket. "If you had come earlier, you'd have been even luckier. We could have gathered lots right from the nests."

"Why should I help you gather eggs?"

"Don't be an idiot. Cook came out not more than half an hour ago and collected the ones that were laid yesterday. I watched her from the thicket. She had to roll them into her apron because I have the basket. And there were lots and lots."

"You have two baskets. You could have left one for her to use, to be considerate."

"You really are an idiot. You still don't get it. I needed her basket in my hand as my excuse for being out here, because I didn't know you'd bring a stoat, how could I? And the old, tired basket you're carrying doesn't count. Cook put it in the bin of stuff for charity. But I fetched it out when I hatched my plan. Hatched, ha! Did you get that at least? Did you get my joke?"

"It's not very clever."

"Well, neither are you apparently."

"I have no idea what you're talking about."

"Obviously. You see, I wasn't thinking about being considerate to Cook or not. I was thinking about my plan. I almost gave up on you, like I did on the other days. If I had, I would have returned the basket to where Cook keeps it and she wouldn't have used her apron. But for some reason I waited longer for you today." She looked at me expectantly.

I hated when she did that. "Oh."

"You should say thank you."

"Thank you for waiting for me."

"And for the egg."

"The egg?" I looked down at the perfect egg inside the basket. "This egg is mine?"

Miss Susanna smirked. "What would I do with it?"

"And I can take it away?"

"That's the point."

Little Paddy loved eggs. "Thank you!"

"Well, I'll stay outside the door just in case. If I see Cook coming this way, I'll quick snatch the stoat and run to her and say I killed it with a rock, and she'll think I'm a heroine—I saved the hens from the nasty stoat. Ha! Normally, that's the dogs' job, to keep out whoever doesn't belong here. But today it will have been me. So Cook will make me a treat at the midday meal."

"She always makes you whatever you want, no matter what you do."

"You don't know that."

"But it's true, isn't it?"

"Maybe. I guess it is. But I never tire of it, so it's always a treat."

Miss Susanna wasn't making sense, but it didn't matter. "I need to talk with you."

"Not now. Not here. You have to walk along the wall, staying low down, so Mrs. Cothran doesn't notice you from a window. She hardly ever looks out the window anyway, but still. Search the wall all along here, on the inside, and you'll find more."

"More what?"

"Eggs, you idiot. Hens don't all take to the nesting boxes. Don't you know anything? Some of them drop their eggs near the wall. And when they roll them . . ." She tilted her head. "You do know hens roll their eggs, don't you?"

I was sure I knew more about hens than Miss Susanna did. Looking after ours had been my job, after all. I nodded.

"Well, good. Anyway, sometimes the rolled eggs get stuck in crevices. Go gather them."

"Why?"

"For you to take back to all your friends, why else?"

Eggs. Ten, no, twelve hens. That meant there could be lots of eggs. My breath came short. This was her plan—this was what I could see forming in her eyes last time! Amazing. But, oh . . . "Cook doesn't know?"

Miss Susanna frowned. "What do you think?"

I stiffened up and felt all hot inside. "No matter what you think of us Irish, I don't steal."

"Steal? I'm giving them to you. We have lots more than we need, all because of you."

"What are you talking about?"

"The spuds. I feed them to the hens, and they've been laying all the time, all of them. So some of the eggs should be yours. Especially the ones in the walls. Cook never collects eggs outside the nesting boxes, because she says we can't be sure how old they are."

"So you're giving us rotten eggs?"

"Stop it."

"Stop what?"

"Stop thinking I'm not nice."

"Why?"

"Because I am nice." She pushed her lips forward and her bottom lip quivered. "I guess I should have smashed all the eggs that were lying around the day I last saw you. Then the ones you found now would have been at most a few weeks old. I didn't think it through." Her eyes clouded and she looked like she was going to cry.

"Eggs last outside in this weather for weeks and weeks," I said softly. "Months, even. Thank you for the eggs. You made a good plan."

Miss Susanna smiled. "I did, didn't I?"

"And I knew you were nice."

"You did not."

"Yes, I did. I was coming here to talk to you, to see if we could . . . hatch . . . a plan together. Some way to feed us all. I didn't have anywhere else to put my hope. I was counting on you. That means I knew you were nice. Deep down, I knew."

Miss Susanna looked away, and if it weren't so shaded inside this coop, I'd have been sure she was blushing. Then she smiled at me again. "Go gather those eggs. You can come every day for them. Just come early—so I can expect you."

"I will." Then I realized . . . "What about the dogs? Won't they come after me?"

"I've been locking them in the dungeon every morning. I only let them out once I give up on you coming that day. I can keep doing that."

"What's a dungeon?"

"Where they used to keep prisoners."

"That sounds horrid. The poor dogs."

"It's not horrid. They think it's a treat, because they usually aren't allowed to go upstairs. The dungeon's in the tower, high up."

"Oh."

"Go on, now. Gather eggs. Feed your brother. Feed your friends."

I looked down at the basket that might be full soon. "Thank you."

"You already thanked me. But words aren't enough."

My breath quickened. This girl always seemed to have her own motives. "What do you mean?"

"Each time you gather eggs, you have to come back to the thicket with me afterwards so we can play. We'll have parties together. I'll tell Cook to make whatever you want. It'll be fun."

What was the matter with her that she still didn't understand? "I can't eat without my friends. Ever again. It's too wrong."

"If you don't, I'll tell Dad I saw a girl stealing eggs from the henhouse. And I'll describe you. I'm very good at describing."

Miss Susanna didn't understand anything. No wonder she had hardly any friends back home.

I shook my head. "Here you go and give us eggs, but you ruin it all with your threats."

"No I don't. The others will still have their eggs. But I'll have you. We'll have so much fun, you'll forget the others. We'll be best friends."

CHAPTER FOURTEEN

Walls

I searched along the walls, wiping at my eyes as I went. There was no reason to cry, so I sure wasn't going to. Miss Susanna was right: Everyone would get eggs. That's what mattered. I had to stop crying. Besides, the wind kept blowing my tears back at me so they cut my face. I wiped hard.

These walls were gray from a distance like all walls, but with my face close, I saw the white spots and the bright yellow ones. I ran my hand gently, gently over the lichen. The white spots were sort of like flattened balls with holes in the middle. The yellow were like little fuzzy buttons. Walls like these marked separations of lands in all directions as far as anyone could walk, because these gray stones were everywhere in Ireland; you didn't have to be rich to build a wall. Some places in the world had only dirt and some had only sand. But Ireland had stones. When Granny was a girl, and even as a woman with children, with Da and Uncle Odran, she went once a year to a stone chapel on Saint Macdara's Island for some festival. It wasn't far from her home on Inis Mór, but no one went to that special little island except at festival time because there was nothing to do, no one to see. Granny loved the stone chapel there. She said it had been built over a thousand years before and she bet it would still be standing over a thousand years hence.

Irish stones lasted. Nothing could destroy them. Even when the most savage winds knocked over parts of a wall, all you had to do was put the stones back in place again. And they were beautiful. The way they fit together felt right, like that's how it was always supposed to be. And the lichen felt right. Everything was right. I wiped at my eyes.

And I spied an egg. I looked around. Miss Susanna was on the other side of the henhouse, so I couldn't see her. And if anyone was watching from the castle, I couldn't tell. Miss Susanna didn't own the hens, so she didn't own the eggs. So she had no right to give them to me. But this egg had been abandoned here, and so, even though Miss Susanna was wrong in more ways than I could figure out, she was right about this: Taking abandoned eggs wasn't stealing. I was sure Ma would agree to that—she would say there was no shame in this. I put it in the basket fast. And there was another. And, oh, another.

I gathered eggs, counting as I went. We were sixteen kids, me included, now that the others had died. And there were eight parents. So I needed exactly two dozen eggs. And I got them. But who knew how long they had been here? Maybe half of them were rotten. Maybe more. So I left the basket in one place and just kept searching and gathering and bringing eggs back to the basket. Eggs and eggs. Thank goodness for the guard dogs; without them the stoat might have eaten all these.

Soon the basket was full, and that was a pity, really, because there were still eggs in the wall, I was sure. But I had no way to haul off the extras. So I wrapped both arms around the basket and carried it carefully through the gap in the wall, passing the dead stoat. I headed for the thicket. Then I put the basket down and went back and snatched that stoat again. Cook had never come out. So Miss Susanna didn't need an excuse for being in the henhouse. And I would not let that creature's flesh go to waste.

I ran toward the basket, and a hen came squawking out from under a little shelter formed by the fallen rocks and nearly hidden by scraggly ragwort. An egg sat there. I reached in. The egg was warm and dry. Just laid. Another lucky egg. Sure, there was room for one more. I perched it securely on the pile of eggs in the basket and draped the body of the stoat across the top. That body was a help, actually. It secured the eggs firmly in place.

When I got to the thicket, I went straight for the tree where I'd stashed the hare.

It wasn't there.

"Looking for this?"

I flinched so hard, I nearly dropped the egg basket. "Emmet! What are you doing here?"

Emmet walked over and dangled the hare in my face. His own face was pinched, his eyes narrowed. "I'm the one who gets to ask. What are you doing here?" His voice was like a low growl.

I looked down at the basket meaningfully, then up into his face. I tried not to blink. "Gathering eggs."

"Stealing eggs, you mean."

"They're abandoned in the wall behind the henhouse of the castle. No one wants them except wild things like this stoat."

"Stoat? That's a weasel." He shook the hare in my face. "And this is a hare. And you've been hunting illegally on top of stealing."

"I killed them by accident."

"You did not."

"What do you know anyway? It was an accident. And then what was the point of leaving them to waste?"

"You're going to hell, Lorraine."

"I am not."

"You are. And not for stealing and hunting. For much worse. I'm onto you, you know. I've been onto you for a while. You've been eating and not sharing."

My knees felt like they would buckle. My whole body shook.

"We've all noticed that you're not as skinny as the rest of us. You don't seem sick at all. My ma says it's because God has marked you as special. And I wanted to believe her." He leaned over the egg basket and put his face in mine. "But she's wrong."

Now he walked around me slowly, swinging the hare, like our priest swinging the thurible. I winced every time it hit me.

"I knew. I suspected it when you offered to be the one to choose who got the giving. You didn't hesitate to give up your chance."

"I was trying to be good," I whispered.

"You were trying to ease your guilt." Emmet stopped in front of me. "And I knew it for sure when you carried a whole basket of kelp in just one hand and shared another basket in the other hand with Paddy. I'm the strongest, and you've never even been close to as strong as me. But now you are, 'cause everyone's so weak." He glared at me. "'Cause we're starving and you're not."

I wanted to put my hands over my ears, but I was holding the basket.

"And the very worst part is…" Emmet's whole face wrinkled with disgust. "The very worst is that you didn't even share with your little brother. Paddy's as bad off as Aeden. They're both in a terrible way. Ma says your little brother—yours!—is beyond hope. We can all see it. And you don't care."

The air felt suddenly strange. I couldn't see my hands in front of me, like when the fog was really thick. I held out the basket to Emmet. "Take it."

"I will."

"Take it fast."

Emmet took the basket and in the same instant I collapsed to my knees.

"Lorraine! Good, you're still here. Oh!"

Miss Susanna's voice came from behind me. But I didn't even try to look. Nothing made sense. I sank back onto my heels. Then I curled forward and hung there. I didn't care about anything. My head was empty. My whole body was empty.

"Who are you? And what are you doing with Lorraine's eggs? And her hare? And her stoat?"

"These are mine," Emmet said in English.

"You talk funny," said Miss Susanna.

"I'm Irish," said Emmet. "An Irish boy speaking your English. You'd talk funny if you tried to speak my Irish."

"You sound much worse than Lorraine."

"So what? The eggs are mine. Lorraine gave them to me."

"Oh. So you're one of her friends? She was bringing that basket back to her friends. But she didn't tell me you were waiting for her here."

I felt a hand grab my shoulder.

"Lorraine, I told you not to bring your friends here. I told you never to do that!"

I sat upright. The fog inside my head had cleared. There was Miss Susanna's face all cross and spluttering. "I didn't bring him here." I did a lot of other bad things. But I didn't do that.

"So how did he get here, then?"

"Ask him."

"How did you get here, boy?"

"I'm Emmet."

"So?"

The two of them just stared at each other. What a stupid impasse.

"So," I said. "That's his name. Emmet. You should say yours now. But you're gone in the head, and you don't know when you're being rude. So I'll introduce you. Emmet, this is my friend Miss Susanna."

"I'm not rude," said Miss Susanna to me.

"Yes you are. You call me names. And you order me around. And right then you criticized Emmet when he's doing you a favor, speaking your language. That was rude. Sometimes you're so rude all I want to do is run away."

Miss Susanna's face had turned red. "So why do you stay?"

"That's what friends do."

She blinked. "You're on my dad's land," she said to Emmet. "Trespassing. It's illegal."

"I'm not trespassing. I'm a cottier's son."

"What's that mean?"

"My da works for Lorraine's da, who works for your da."

"Oh. Well, what are you doing up here, away from the fields?"

"I followed Lorraine."

I stared at Emmet. How had he followed me? I'd left home at barely dawn. And he couldn't have known I'd be going up over the hill today . . . no one knew that. Had he been following me for days? Weeks? But I didn't care. Not really. What did it matter?

"Why?"

"Because she's rotten."

"What do you mean?"

"She's been eating. Eating and not sharing. So I've been following her to find out where she gets food from. I saw her kill the weasel and the hare. She threw a big rock on them. And I waited back in the grasses when she came into these woods. After a while I crept in, all quiet-like, and she was gone, but the hare was in the tree. So I knew she would come back this way and I waited for her." Emmet put the basket on the ground and pointed at it. "And she came back with this basket." He puffed out his chest. "She's a criminal. Larceny—that's what she's guilty of." His eyes met mine. "We both know the word now: larceny." He looked back at Miss Susanna. "Lorraine is going to hell for not sharing her food."

Miss Susanna shook her head. "You've got it all wrong."

"What would you know? Pampered puss face. We're in a terrible way. Nola died. And then Deirdre and Quinlin and Riley. And he was my best friend." Emmet's voice broke. "They died of the fever, but it still falls on Lorraine." He looked at me.

I shook my head no.

"It does, because if you had shared your stolen food with those fever-ridden beggars in the first place, Riley's family never would have had to take them into their home." Emmet turned to Miss Susanna. "You see? It's Lorraine's fault. And Aeden and Paddy are failing now. And that's really from starvation. Paddy's her brother. Did you know that? Did you know how bad Lorraine is?"

Miss Susanna's mouth had come open. Now she took a breath that swelled her chest and she touched her fingers to her lips. "Four of you have died? It really happened? Lorraine said it would, but I thought she was exaggerating. All Irish do." She bent over me. "And two more are dying? Paddy's dying? Paddy, the little brother you're supposed to take care of?"

I wouldn't say it. I would never say my brother was dying. I wouldn't let it happen. Never.

Miss Susanna stood up straight. "Well, Emmet," she said at last, "Lorraine is not as bad as you say. She didn't steal the eggs and she didn't hunt those animals. But she did eat without sharing with you all."

"See?" said Emmet. "That's the worst. Friends don't do that. Friends take care of each other."

"But only two times—she ate with me and didn't share with you only two times. And only because . . ." She pressed her lips together. Then she lifted her chin. "Because I wouldn't allow her to."

"What?"

"I invited her to my party. And I wouldn't let her take food away."

"Party?"

"I have parties with my dollies. And, oh!" She reached inside the pouch that hung from the sash at her waist. "I almost forgot again. Here." She dangled something pink in front of my face.

I took it and turned it over in my hands. It was a tiny pink jumper.

"It's for Margaret the Bone. Did you bring her?"

"I forgot."

"Well, remember next time. And put that pink jumper on her. I asked Cook to make it. I forgot to give it to you before in all the excitement over the eggs, so when I remembered, I came running after you."

It was far too big for skinny Margaret. But I could stuff dry grasses inside. I could make her look plump, like Granny used to do. I loved it. "Thank you."

"You're welcome. So, Emmet." Miss Susanna looked Emmet full in the face. "It's me you should be mad at, not Lorraine. She wanted to bring back food for all of you. But I wouldn't let her. She had to keep everything about me a secret. Dad would get furious if he found out I was spending time with an Irish girl. So I threatened Lorraine so she wouldn't tell."

Emmet furrowed his brows. "But you let her take the eggs, and you said she was taking them for us."

"She convinced me that you all really needed food, and besides, the eggs were just going to waste."

Emmet looked at me. "Is this true?"

I nodded.

"*Maith*—good," said Emmet switching to Irish. "Ye girl ye! Because I hated it when I suspected you. You were always my second favorite, after Riley."

"You were my second favorite, after Deirdre." And that was the truth.

"You're not going to hell," said Emmet. "I'm sorry I said that."

"I hope I'm not going to hell. But if I can't go to heaven, at least I hope I die in Ireland."

"Me too," said Emmet. "I wouldn't die anywhere else."

Emmet tipped his head to me, then turned to Miss Susanna and crossed his arms over his chest. "It seems to me that we've got the advantage over you," he said in English.

"How's that?"

"All we need to do is tell your father you play with Lorraine, and you'll be in trouble. So now we can force you to keep helping us."

"No you can't," said Miss Susanna.

"And why not?"

I got to my feet. "Because you can't force someone who has already decided to keep helping." I looked at Miss Susanna.

She gave one of those quick nods of hers. "That's what friends do, after all."

CHAPTER FIFTEEN

Eggs

Ma sat at the table with me across from her and little Paddy at her side. "Egg and onion and kale scramble," said Ma. "It'll be like a feast. We just have to go through these eggs and find enough good ones before Da and Emmet get back with the crowd." She smiled as she took an egg and dropped it gently into a pot of cold water. It sank to the bottom. "A good one. Very fresh." She wiped it dry and put it in our own old egg basket. That's where we were saving the freshest ones, for future use.

Paddy was already eating a soft mush of egg poached in buttermilk. His big, steady eyes showed he was concentrating on the job of chewing and swallowing. I hated how hollow his cheeks were, how yellow his skin had turned.

"Can I do the next one?" I asked.

Ma passed me an egg. I put my hand down into the nearly icy water and let go. The egg sank, but then stood on the bottom on its pointy end.

"Good," said Ma. "But it needs to be used fast." She took it out and cracked it into the big bowl. "Let's pray there are enough like this to make today's feast without delving into the really fresh ones."

"That way we can feast again tomorrow," said little Paddy, echoing what Ma had said earlier.

I smiled at him. It was good to know he was listening. I got on my knees on the stool and leaned across the table and kissed him on the top of the head. His hair still smelled of smoke. It had been two weeks since we'd burned that hut, but he reeked of it.

"Maybe not tomorrow," said Ma. "Maybe the next day. But you, my dearest, will get an egg tomorrow if there are any left at all, I promise you that."

"Why me?" said little Paddy.

Ma's face went slack.

"Because you're the littlest," I said quickly. "That's the rule."

"Indeed," said Ma. She picked up the next egg and frowned. "Oh, dear. Just feel. It's that little bit lighter." She handed it to me.

I wasn't sure I could feel a difference, maybe just the slightest. I dropped it in the water. It floated.

"See?"

I took the rotten egg and went to Muc, who had been standing by the hearth watching us. I rolled the egg to her. Muc gobbled it up and then came to stand beside the table, her beady eyes on my hands.

"Look," said little Paddy. "There's a hole in that egg."

Ma took the egg and her face lit up. She crumpled an old piece of cloth and set it on the table right in front of little Paddy and nestled the egg in it. Then she went back to sorting eggs.

A tiny noise came from the egg. Little Paddy laughed. I did too. I wondered if this was the final egg I'd found—the lucky one behind the ragwort. That hen I'd disturbed might have been sitting on it for days. Ha!

"I'm going to see it hatch," said little Paddy. "I'll see it take its first steps." He laughed again. "Can it be mine, Ma? My pet?"

Ma cracked an egg into the big bowl. "If it really hatches, Paddy, and if we can keep it alive, by mid-spring it will be ready to eat. And we'll eat it."

"Even if it's my pet?"

"Even if it's your pet." Ma dropped another egg into the cold water. "Meat is too precious, Paddy. You're old enough to understand that. Do you? Do you understand?" She cracked that egg into the big bowl.

Little Paddy's face was solemn. "I do."

"Then it can be your pet." Ma put an egg in the water. It floated. She handed it to me and I fed it from my hand to Muc. "But don't count on it hatching. It was out in the cold. It's probably weaker than it should be. It might not even have the strength to peck its way out."

"I'll help it," said little Paddy. "I can crack the egg open."

Ma cracked another egg into the big bowl. "We don't know how long the chick has been working at hatching yet. Let's give him till midday tomorrow. If he's not hatched by then, you and I can try to help him out. In the meantime, we need to keep him warm."

"I'll hold him inside my shirt. Against my belly."

Ma wiped off the egg that had just sunk to the bottom and put it in our egg basket. "That's a good idea. Finish your food first. Then you can do that."

We sorted all the eggs. Amazingly, only a few were rotten. Ma said the unusually cold weather would have preserved any that were laid in the past few months. So something good had come of this perishing autumn and winter. Our egg basket was half-full of truly fresh eggs, and the big bowl was full of cracked eggs, ready to be scrambled.

Ma chopped the kale while I dropped the onions in the cold water. Then she passed me the knife and I chopped those onions. The fumes hurt my eyes less after the onions had been in water, but somehow that trick didn't work for Ma. So the job of chopping onions always fell to Da or me.

I had just finished when the door opened and Da led in the crowd. Teagan had Noreen by one hand, while her ma held on to Sheelagh and her da held on to Carrick. Fiona had Neil by one hand, while her da had Murray by the hand and her ma held Aeden in her arms. Corey and Iona held on to each other. Last to come in were Alana, and her ma holding Kyla by the hand, and her da holding Kearney by the hand, and Emmet at the rear, holding on to no one. I looked across the whole crowd and realized they were huddled together in families. They looked hesitant, even a bit scared. It must have felt odd for them to be in our cottage all at once. They'd been inside before, of course, but never all of them at once. They barely fit.

Da shooed Muc out the door and said, "Sit down, everyone."

But they just stood there.

"You might as well take a seat on the floor," I said. "Wherever you can find a spot. I swept it good before you came." The sweeping was true, but silly to say. Earthen floors were never truly clean, no matter how hard you packed them. Plus, most of the cottiers were dirtier than our floor on its worst days.

In a murmur of thanks they settled down, pressing together tight to keep a distance from the table. None of them had furniture in their huts, so even our single table and few stools seemed luxurious to them—and intimidating.

It was just as well. Little Paddy still sat at the table, both hands protectively over the egg cradled inside his shirt against his tummy. I was glad no one was close enough to bump his arm.

Da was on the floor now, like everyone else. Ma was already stirring eggs and vegetables in the pan. Then she and I went together from person to person, putting a scoop of the scrambled mess into the bowls they'd all brought and held out now. When we finished, we served ourselves and sat by Da. People ate in silence, the only noise being the scrape of spoons against the tin bowls.

"I need to understand," said Teagan's da, at last. "I won't risk going to prison. Exactly where did these eggs come from?"

"It's a bit late to ask," said Fiona's da, and he forced a laugh.

"I'm still asking, late or not."

Da poked my arm. "Go ahead, Lorraine."

I stood up and looked at Emmet. He stood up too, and picked his way carefully past people to come stand beside me.

"We have a secret source," I said. "We're not stealing. We're not doing anything that hurts anyone."

"No larceny," said Emmet.

"What source?" said Teagan's da.

"We can't tell you," said Emmet. "That's why it's secret."

"And we have to trust you? Two kids?"

"Two good kids," said Emmet's da.

"And they confided in me," said Da. "And in Catherine."

"Why won't they confide in all of us?"

"Because they're protecting someone. They're keeping a confidence, as anyone who makes a promise should. We back them up."

"No offense, Francis," said Teagan's ma, "but a wild goose never reared a tame gosling."

"Exactly how am I wilder than any other Irishman?" said Da.

"You're the one who led the others to the strand instead of to mass a month ago. I'm not forgetting that, I'm not. You're the one whose family didn't show up for mass on Christmas morning, when those kiddies of yours sure needed it."

"There's nothing dishonest about not going to mass, even on Christmas morning," said Da. "I am an honest man. And I swear to you, what Emmet and Lorraine are doing is honest. Is that enough for you?"

"That's enough for me," said Teagan's da.

Teagan's ma looked down.

"This source of eggs," said Fiona's da, "how reliable is it? How many eggs can you get? How often?"

"We don't know." I pressed against Emmet.

"Any eggs, even now and then, are better than no eggs," said Emmet. He pressed back against me.

"So, as far as you know," said Fiona's da, "these could be the last eggs we eat."

"I guess. If nothing we hope for works out."

"That's not true," said Ma quickly. "There's a half basket of good eggs left. We can have another egg meal in a few days. We can do it all again."

"Twice, then," said Fiona's da. "Maybe twice and never again. Is that right, Catherine?"

Ma sighed. "Maybe."

"That's what I thought. Next time you do your egg meal, you can make it stretch further," said Fiona's da, "because we won't be here."

"What do you mean?" said Da.

"We're going to Glasgow. Leaving on the ship from Galways just shy of a week from now."

Da shook his head. "Jobs for Irish are scarce in Glasgow. My brother Odran told me."

"Adamina's family is taking us in till we get jobs. It'll work out. Nothing's working out here."

I looked at Fiona. She was staring at her da. So were Iona and Corey and Murray and Neil. All of them. Could this be the first they were hearing of these plans?

I looked at their ma. She sat there with little Aeden on her lap, stroking his hair. He wasn't looking anywhere. He was listless. Like little Paddy was most of the time.

"Things will change," said Da. "Next autumn maybe there

will be no murrain. Maybe we'll have spuds from August to April, in plenty. We will, I bet. The murrain can't come three years in a row. It just can't."

"It can," said Fiona's da.

"You said it, not God," said Ma.

"Even if there isn't any murrain next August," said Fiona's da, "we'll starve. Think about it, Francis, Catherine. We have no spuds to plant this coming spring. How can there be a harvest if there's nothing to plant?"

Da stared at him.

I was hugging myself. We hadn't saved haws for planting— there was just too little food to do that. But we'd gouged out buds before we cooked our spuds, and saved those disk-shaped portions for spring planting. Da said that would work. Now, though, the look on his face told me he didn't know for sure. It was all just hope. I felt sick inside.

"You see?" said Fiona's ma. "We have to think of the children. They can't go without spuds that long. We have nothing in Ireland. But we have family in Scotland. My family."

We didn't have family anywhere, or not anywhere that could help us. Uncle Odran had never married. And Ma's family was dead. There were distant cousins here and there, but no place that was any better off than we were here. We couldn't go move in with family even if we'd wanted to.

"The ships are dangerous, I hear," said Emmet's da. "Not enough to eat. Filth. Disease. Many die at sea. They're calling them coffin ships."

"That's the Canada ships," said Fiona's da. "I heard about

them too. The ones that bring over timber and then take on Irish for the return trip, packing them into the places the timber was in. They're hell. The ships to Scotland are different. The trip is far shorter and the ships are made for carrying people. They're better." He looked across his children's staring faces. "They're good. We'll be safe."

Iona turned her face away, and I could see straight into her eyes: terror. I'd be feeling the same. Even if she survived the ship, who knew what Scotland was really like? If I had been sitting near her, I'd have hugged her. Instead, I hugged myself.

At last someone stirred and they were all getting up, all brushing off their bottoms, all crowding to the door in a spiritless shuffle. Then the door opened and the night came alive. The northern lights danced everywhere. Deepest purple fading to pink, yellow shooting up through it and a bright blue halo arching across the whole thing, then darkest indigo beyond.

"The Irish sky," said someone. "You got to love it."

Someone small was crying.

Emmet stood beside me. "There's northern lights in Glasgow, too," he said loudly, for all to hear.

"How do you know?" I whispered in his ear.

"There has to be," he whispered back. "Nothing could be that unfair." And he marched off into the night with the rest of them.

CHAPTER SIXTEEN

Chicks

Y ou're not sleeping, Paddy, and I know it," came Ma's loud
whisper. "Da's finished his telling and he's already sleeping. I'm long done singing. It's time for all of us. You shut
your eyes and stop all that rolling around, now."

"I can't sleep."

"And why not?"

"The egg."

"I told you, you cannot sleep with it."

"But it'll get cold and die."

"It's on the table in the cloth, Paddy. It's warm."

"Maybe that's not warm enough."

"I can't move it closer to the hearth, you know that. I told
you. It could be too warm. The poor little thing could cook."

"See? The egg needs me. He needs my body heat. It's just
right."

"You'll crush him, and then think how sad you'll be."

I sat up. "I'll hold him all night."

"Yay!" said little Paddy.

"You can't do that, Lorraine. You need your sleep as much
as Paddy does."

"I'm not sleeping a wink with him tossing and turning as

it is." I got up and went to the table. I sat down and cupped my hands around the egg. "Go to sleep now, Paddy."

"You stay awake, Lorraine," he said.

"I will."

"Promise?"

"I promise."

"Thank you, Lorraine."

"My children are gone in the head," said Ma with a sigh.

Within moments, the room was full of the sounds of sleep. On and on they slept, while I stared at nothing. But I was glad to be up. I had an idea, and I needed to think about it, because it hurt. I looked around the dim room and listened to the small cracks of the fire and breathed deep of the peat smoke and tried to figure out what I was going to do. I knew what I should do, what would be good and kind, what would be generous. But it was hard to think about generosity these days. And the night seemed to hold no answers. It passed far too slowly.

When it had to be near dawn, I put my mouth to the egg. "What do you think, little chick?"

Oh! I could feel the movement inside. I held the shell in one palm and rubbed it lightly with the other palm and I breathed my hot breath on it.

"Come on, little chick. You can do it."

Crack. And, look! A little beak peeked out of the new hole. And now there was a series of holes and the egg rocked in my palm. I walked careful, careful, holding the egg-chick close to my chest, over to where little Paddy lay asleep. I tickled his neck with my toes.

He rolled away.

I kicked his little butt.

He groaned and sat up. "Lorraine?"

"He's hatching. Come."

Little Paddy got up faster than I thought he could move. We walked over near the hearth, where there was the most light from the fire, and I set the egg on the ground. No sooner had we sat down than one whole half of the shell cracked off and the chick flopped out on his back.

Little Paddy laughed.

The chick jumped around like a crazed thing, and I was so glad we hadn't left him on the table all on his own. He'd have fallen off for sure. He flopped this way and that, trying to get his footing. His wet feathers turned gold as he stretched his neck and wings. He was wonderful—totally grand.

Finally he stood there, one big eye looking at us, then he turned his head the other way and the other big eye looked at us. "He's darling," I said.

"Pointy," said little Paddy.

"He's not pointy. He's fluffy. Or he's getting fluffy, as he dries."

"It's his name," said little Paddy. "Pointy."

"But your hedgehog's name is Pointy. You can't have two pets named Pointy. Imagine if they learned their names. You'll call, 'Pointy!' and they'll both come running."

"How did you know Pointy became my pet?"

"I saw you playing with him."

"That was long ago. He's gone now."

"Oh. I'm sorry, Paddy."

"Don't be. Now I have Pointy."

"You do," said Ma. I hadn't realized she'd woken. "It's amazing he survived. The question now is how we're going to feed him."

"He can eat turnip greens," I said. "And dried kale. And I'll find him grasses he'll like."

"That's good, Lorraine. But he needs grains—finely ground—some real meal. Don't worry, we've got a few days to figure that out. He doesn't need to eat immediately, no matter what." She scooped up Pointy and put him in the old egg basket that Miss Susanna had given me. Then she put the basket on the shelf over the hearth. "He can stay there, cozy and safe, while we get going. It's morning, and our friends are starting their journey early. Wake your da. Get ready."

And so we went, the four of us, through the shivery dawn, to gather at the cottiers' huts and say good-bye to Fiona's family. If they had managed to scrape together the money just a little bit sooner, they could have left from Clifden quay. But now all the ships were full for months. It seemed no sooner was a ship-sailing announced than it was full. And Fiona's da refused to wait, so they'd had to buy tickets leaving from Galways. Ma explained that it would take them three days to walk to Galways if they were lucky, but their da was allowing them four just in case.

Da rolled little Paddy in our old handcart. It had only two wheels, one in the middle of each side. So when you let go of the handles, it slanted one way or the other. The bottom and handles were blue. The sides and wheels were red. It was in dire need of repainting. When we got to the cottiers' huts, Da planted the cart in front of Fiona's da and lifted out little Paddy. "This will come in handy," he said.

"I can't take that." Fiona's da shook his head. "No, I can't."

"I haven't used it since the harvest of '44," said Da. "The last good harvest. If I ever need a cart again, it will mean good times are back. So I'll be able to buy another one."

Fiona's da shook his head again, but her ma put a staying hand on her husband's arm. "Thank you, Francis," she said, looking Da full in the face. "The children can take turns riding with Aeden. It'll be a grand help."

"I'll sell it in Galways before I get on the ship," said Fiona's da. "And once I'm in Glasgow, I'll find a way to get the money back to you."

"There's no rush," said Da. He slapped Fiona's da on the back.

Ma handed Fiona's ma a cloth tied up like a satchel.

She raised her eyebrows in question.

"Eggs," said Ma. "Hard-boiled. I kept one back for Paddy. But we all agreed the rest should go to you, for the journey to Galways."

When had the rest of us agreed on that? I quick looked around. Though everyone's face was pinched with hunger, the other mas and das were nodding in agreement. Ma was right; no one resented the loss of the eggs.

I bet that was because they trusted we'd get more, Emmet and me, because that's what we said we'd do. And we would. We had to.

I tried to catch Emmet's eye. He was talking to Murray, fast and earnest. Murray was saying they'd be eating haggis soon, acting all brave like the oldest boy should, and Emmet was actually saying that was grand, haggis was grand. I could feel how much Emmet was going to miss Murray. I looked at Fiona. She was looking at the ground. She hadn't raised her eyes at all this morning, so far as I had seen. Of course not—she was trying her best not to cry. And that thought made my eyes sting. Oh, I'd miss her as much as Emmet would miss Murray. And I'd miss Iona. And Corey and Murray and Neil and little Aeden. I'd miss all of them. Just as much as I missed Deirdre and Riley and Quinlin and baby Nola. So many gone.

Our world was coming apart. And it didn't have to be this way. There were folks to blame for this. English folks. Fiona and Murray and Iona and Corey and Neil and little Aeden—all of them could stay right here, where they belonged, if only the English would share what they'd stolen from us in the first place.

But I mustn't think that way, because if I did, it would show on my face and that wouldn't be good for anyone. Fiona's family would stay alive in Scotland. That was the most important thing. Fair or unfair—who cared, so long as they lived.

And we would stay alive here in Ireland. We had to.

We would, wouldn't we?

For a fleeting moment—just three seconds—I had the urge to latch onto Fiona and go with her. Despite the terror of traveling on a ship, there was something marvelous about arriving in another land, getting a fresh start. It would be grand to escape the specter of starvation. I actually envied her.

But I'd never leave my family. And none of us would ever leave Ireland. This was home—this beautiful green land. We had to stay here and take care of her. Her past, her present, her future—they were entrusted to us. Like Uncle Odran had said: Ireland belonged to the Irish. And if we didn't stand and fight for her, maybe we didn't deserve her. She needed us. Every country needed her citizens. That's how it was. That's how it had to be.

Already Fiona's da had taken up the cart handles and little Aeden sat in it, holding on to the sides with hands so white they seemed almost transparent. They had to be cold as ice.

I went up and whispered to him, "Sit on your hands. That'll keep them warmer."

He stared at me with eyes as big in his head as the new chick's eyes, and he whispered, "I don't want to fall out."

"You won't."

"I never rode in a cart before."

"I used to ride in this cart all the time when I was little. Littler than you. And I never fell out. Sit on your hands, Aeden. Keep them warm."

Aeden chewed on his bottom lip. But he kept holding on to the sides of the cart.

Then everyone was hugging and kissing and promising to take care.

Murray took a cart handle from his da.

"You want to pull first?" asked the da.

"Nah. Let Corey and Neil. While they're fresh. I'll pull after they tire out. Then you can pull."

"Good thinking," said the da.

Corey and Neil each took a handle, looking solemn and proud.

Corey looked at Iona. "You want your turn riding with Aeden?"

Iona shook her head. "Later. When I tire out." She looked at Murray. "Right?"

"Right."

"Then I suppose we can put our satchels in the cart with Aeden," said Fiona, finally coming to life. "There's room."

So in went the satchel of eggs that her ma had passed to her. And in went the satchels that Murray and their ma and da were carrying. From the shapes of them, I guessed they held turnips and cabbages.

Iona took her ma's hand and they started off along the boreen that led to the main road.

"May the road rise to meet you," called Teagan's ma. And we all joined in, saying the Irish blessing, the most beautiful blessing anywhere ever. It made a chill go up my spine, I loved it so much.

It was now or never. My eyes burned. I ran and caught up to them and touched Iona's shoulder. She turned to me and I quick put Margaret the Bone in her hands. "For you."

"To keep?" said Iona. "Really?"

"Are you sure?" said her ma.

I nodded. I'd thought about this most of the night, thinking I was sure, thinking I wasn't sure at all. I couldn't think anymore.

Iona hugged Margaret the Bone tight. "She's so pretty. I was afraid to look at her before. I saw her in your hands and I wouldn't look, because she's so pretty."

And she was, all snug in the pink jumper Miss Susanna's cook had made, stuffed with grasses, little purple flowers peeking out around the wrists. I'd picked them that morning as we walked the boreen. I touched the flowers.

"Sweet coltsfoot," said Iona. "My favorite."

"They're her favorite too," I said.

Iona laughed. "Good, then Margaret and I have something in common right off."

"How did you know her name was Margaret?"

"Fiona told me."

"Now, Margaret," I said to the doll I loved, "you take good care of Iona. You show her everything beautiful that there is to see in Scotland. And when the red poppies bloom . . ." I hesitated. But then I thought of Emmet—Scotland had to have red poppies in spring too, anything else would be too unfair. "When they bloom, you decorate her hair with them."

Iona kissed my cheek. "Bye-bye, Lorraine. Margaret will think about you every day."

CHAPTER SEVENTEEN

Cold

"Wait up, Emmet."

He slowed, but he didn't stop. "Catch up."

The ground had turned so cold in the week since I'd last seen Miss Susanna, it was hardly bearable. I'd tied old cloths around my feet this morning. Without them, I'd be crying now. But the cloths made me hobble. Emmet's feet were totally bare. How on earth could he go that fast? Was he made of iron? And how did he remember so well which way to go? He'd only been there once before, but he never hesitated.

My feet felt like knives—a hundred at the least—were cutting into them. If I had realized Emmet knew how to get back to the castle on his own, I'd have let him go alone. What was the point of both of us going, anyway?

I concentrated on looking at the trees. Each one of them. I could always get past one more tree. Anyone could do that. So that's all the distance I set for myself: one tree at a time. When I reached this one, then I'd set my goals on the next one.

Finally we were there and Miss Susanna was waiting for us.

"Here." She took two dollies out of her carriage and put them in Emmet's arms. They were Geraldine and Eleanor. Glorious dollies.

"What?"

"Just hold them."

Emmet held Geraldine and Eleanor gingerly, as if they might break. I was sure he'd never touched anything so grand in his life, for I hadn't, and he was poorer than me. Why was Miss Susanna entrusting them to Emmet? I watched her. The look on her face told me that she was up to something again. But she was such an odd duck, it was impossible to guess what.

Miss Susanna took the old egg basket that was over my arm and put the third doll in my arm in its place. Alexandra. I was partial to Alexandra; she was the doll who had allowed me to eat her portion the first time I'd had a feast with Miss Susanna. In my eyes, she was the prettiest.

Miss Susanna put the basket on the ground, stood tall, and rubbed her gloved hands together as though she was ready for business.

Gloves. What a luxury were gloves. I squeezed Alexandra against my side with my arm and put my hands in front of my mouth and breathed hot on them.

Suddenly Miss Susanna's face changed; she looked annoyed. "Did you forget Margaret the Bone again? I brought Alexandra and Geraldine and Eleanor just so they could meet her. I mean, it's too cold for a party. We'd all freeze. But they could have met and kissed at least."

"I didn't forget her."

"So where is she?"

I tightened my whole face so I wouldn't get teary. "On her way to Galways."

"What do you mean?"

"Iona's taking her to Scotland. Once they get to Galways, they'll take a ship to Glasgow. Iona's her new ma now."

"Dressed in my pink jumper?"

"It's not yours. You gave it to me for Margaret. And I gave Margaret to Iona. That's how it goes. The jumper is Margaret's and Margaret is Iona's."

"Why would you do that?"

"You wouldn't understand."

"Who's being rude now?"

She was right. That was rude. "I'm sorry."

"So why did you give her Margaret the Bone with the pretty new jumper?"

"Iona was afraid of going to Scotland. I figured if she brought a bit of Ireland with her, it could help."

"Iona is an idiot, because Scotland is nowhere near as bad as Ireland. Dad took me there once. They have highland cows, with long wavy hair."

I refused to let Miss Susanna rile me. "And mostly, I gave Margaret to Iona because Iona loves her."

"But you do too." Miss Susanna looked hard at me.

I could feel my eyes filling.

"Don't cry."

"I'm not."

"I can see your eyes, Lorraine. But anyway, you were being a good friend. I understand why you gave her Margaret the Bone. See? I understand."

"Saints, have mercy! Could you two stop this now?" said

Emmet. He stepped from foot to foot—which meant his feet were cold too. "Let's get the eggs."

"You can't," said Miss Susanna.

My head got hot. I could hear Fiona's da that first night we ate eggs, asking about the egg supply—how many, how often. What fools we'd been to think this plan would work. We'd eaten eggs once—then given the next to Fiona's family—and that's all!

"And why not?" said Emmet. "Lorraine said there's lots more eggs in the walls."

"There are. But Dad found out I was locking the dogs in the dungeon in the morning, and he forbid me to do it anymore. So the dogs are guarding the walls again. All day long. All night long. That's their job."

"I'm not scared of dogs," said Emmet.

Miss Susanna looked at me. "Is he an idiot?"

"He's brave," I said.

"A brave idiot."

"We need those eggs," said Emmet.

"I know that. I'm not an idiot." Miss Susanna pushed the doll carriage up to Emmet. "Take a peek."

We both peeked. The carriage was full of eggs.

Emmet whooped and kissed my cheek.

"I'm the one who did the work," said Miss Susanna. "So why are you kissing Lorraine? It took me a long time to collect all these. But you're filthy, so I'd never want a thank-you kiss from you anyway."

Emmet's eyes flashed. I quick cleared my throat before he

could say anything nasty to her. "We better start back. It'll be slow going with the carriage."

"You can't take my dolly carriage," said Miss Susanna. "Someone might ask where it is. Cook or Dad. You have to put the eggs in the old egg basket."

I shook my head, though I was already putting Alexandra in Miss Susanna's arms. With both hands I loaded eggs into the basket. "There's far too many. These could fill two baskets. Or more."

"Oh. You're right. Well, then, you can leave the extras here in the thicket and come back for them later."

"Some wild animal will eat them," said Emmet.

"Oh. Well." Miss Susanna looked at me. "We've got a problem."

"Emmet, you stay here and guard the eggs while I take the first batch home."

"Your feet hurt," said Emmet. "You can't make the trip twice."

"Your feet hurt too."

"Not as much as yours."

"Then I'll guard while you go back and forth."

Emmet shook his head. "I won't leave you here getting colder and colder."

"Emmet, we can't afford to lose so many eggs. If we doled them out, say in a big scramble again every other day, this many eggs could last two weeks. Maybe more. Think how strong everyone would get."

Emmet looked at Miss Susanna. "Guard the eggs till I get back."

"I can't."

"You don't know how to be a friend," said Emmet.

Miss Susanna's face went blotchy. I wanted to put my hand over Emmet's mouth.

"I'm truly sorry," she said. "But I can't. I'm going with Dad to visit a friend of his. Another landlord. With a castle as big as ours, Dad says. I'm going so that I can see if they have chickens, and if there's a way to gather their extra eggs. They don't even have a child for me to play with—so I'm doing it just for you. It's all part of the plan. I told you I'd help you. This is how I'm doing it." She spread her hands in explanation. "Be reasonable. You need to eat for more than two weeks, after all."

Emmet just looked at her.

"You're a good friend," I said. "You have good plans. Emmet and I are grateful. We'll figure this out."

"I already have." Emmet put Geraldine and Eleanor into my arms and pulled off his raggedy jumper. His bare chest was bluish white and all his ribs showed. The jumper hardly kept out the wind. That's why he moved so fast, to keep himself as warm as possible. How thick could I be?

Miss Susanna watched him, but she spoke out the side of her mouth to me. "He's got bats in his belfry."

I stared at Emmet with a sick fascination. This had to be leading somewhere—Emmet was cunning. And all at once I knew. Of course.

He tied knots in the cuffs of the jumper sleeves and held it upside down. "A perfect egg satchel."

"You'll freeze," said Miss Susanna.

"Not if I walk fast." Emmet carefully slid eggs down the sleeves of his jumper. Then he loaded up the chest cavity. All the eggs fit.

I looked at Miss Susanna and the answer dawned on me: "Drape your shawl around him."

She shook her head fast. "I can't."

"Of course you can. Your da will buy you a new one just like that."

"No. Dad would ask what happened to it. And when I told him, he'd be so disappointed in me."

"Sometimes you make me want to smack you." But I couldn't waste any more time fighting with her. I quick lay Eleanor and Geraldine in the carriage. "I'll carry the jumper."

"I'll carry it," said Emmet. "It's heavier than the basket."

"But it will be important to walk slow with it, so the eggs don't crack. It's not made for eggs, like the basket is. If it swings too much, we could wind up with a mess. I walk slow. You take the basket and go as fast as you can."

"I'll . . ."

"Just go, Emmet!"

Emmet was already shivering. He took the basket and left.

Miss Susanna grabbed hold of my arm. "Come back tomorrow."

"Not that soon. We won't need more food for a couple of weeks. And I sure wouldn't come back just to see you . . . you and your warm shawl."

Miss Susanna blanched. "You can be so mean sometimes."

"What do you expect, the way you behave? Emmet will be half-frozen by the time he gets back to our cottage."

"With eggs. He'll get back there with eggs. And it was me who gathered them. I couldn't give my shawl. I just couldn't. But I gave the eggs." Her voice trembled and her eyes filled with tears.

"You're right." I patted her hand. I didn't understand her, but somehow I knew she was being the best friend she could be. "I'm sorry I said that."

"Listen, Lorraine. Who knows what I'll find out at the other castle today? There might be nothing for us, and we'll have to make up a new plan. We'll need to talk a lot to do that."

"You're right," I said soothingly. "You're right, you're right. I'll meet you soon. But only if it's not this cold. I can't do this long walk in such perishing cold." I clenched my teeth a moment to keep them from chattering. "Today, halfway here, I didn't think I'd make it the rest of the way."

"Then we can meet in town," said Miss Susanna. "Is that closer for you?"

"Lots. But how will you get to town?"

"Dad will take me."

"On what excuse?"

"I'll figure it out. Meet me at the graveyard at noon tomorrow."

The world seemed so easy for Miss Susanna. "Figuring it out" probably meant telling her da she simply wanted to go to town. Friend or not, I really, really could have smacked her.

The air grew blurry. I rubbed my eyes, but it wouldn't

change. There was white on my hands. It was snowing! It was that cold! But that was good, really. Snow made the ground softer. I had to think about things the right way.

Miss Susanna had turned her face up to the sky and opened her mouth to catch the snowflakes. She was laughing.

"Nothing bothers you," I snapped. "Everything is good for you."

"That's not true. You don't understand, Lorraine. You have your mom and dad and Paddy. And you have Emmet and all the others. I have Dad. He is the only one who loves me. The only one in the world. I can't risk that."

I swallowed the lump that had formed in my throat. "Don't do that."

"What?"

"Don't make me feel sorry for you." I didn't know what had happened to Miss Susanna's ma. And I wouldn't let myself ask. I couldn't afford to think about that. Not now. Not if it meant not asking her to do things for us. "We're the ones that need help, not you." But she'd already gone and done it—she'd already made me sad. I put my palm soft on her cheek. This girl who seemed lonelier than I could even imagine. Was she ever happy?

But still, she did have so much. And, oh, that meant I should ask for more. Miss Susanna could make anything happen. "Let's meet the day after tomorrow, can we? And could you bring me a bag of meal?"

"A bag of meal? Why, those bags are huge. Even Cook can't lift a bag by herself."

"I mean something small. A pound bag. Yellow meal."

"That junk? Dad says it's from Indian corn—from America—not fit for human consumption. We eat good meal—finely ground."

"Any meal will do. Just a small amount. A couple of handfuls."

"What difference would a couple of handfuls make? That won't feed your family."

"It's not for my family. It's for a pet."

"I'm not stealing from Cook's larder to feed your smelly old pets."

"Her name is Susanna."

"Susanna?" Miss Susanna narrowed her eyes. "Whose name is Susanna?"

"The chick that hatched from one of the eggs I gathered last time."

Miss Susanna smiled. "You named a chick after me? A cute little yellow chick?"

I tried not to blink as I nodded. What a fibber I'd become.

"Well, sure. I'll give you the meal for Susanna the Chick when I meet you in town. Day after tomorrow."

CHAPTER EIGHTEEN

Fever

Everyone crowded into our cottage again, tramping in snow on their rag-covered feet and turning the floor sticky. But at least there was more room now, even with Bo Bo standing inside, because we were fewer. Ten children, six adults. I was keeping track. I wasn't glad we were fewer, of course not. But it meant keeping us in eggs would be that much less difficult. It was important to appreciate a full moon on a dark night.

Ma cooked a soft scramble of eggs and buttermilk, with a side of mashed turnips. Teagan helped her serve it. I wasn't allowed to. Ma had a different job in mind for me: feeding Emmet. So she made me go stand and wait beside him, till she could convince his ma to leave him for a bit.

Emmet had arrived at our cottage the day before half-frozen. His feet were like lumps of ice. His whole body shook uncontrollably. Still, not a single egg in his basket had cracked, Ma told me. He'd walked over two miles on that uneven terrain. Sure, it was mostly downhill, but he was barefoot and bare-chested against the winds and snow. And the whole way all he thought of was keeping those eggs safe. Which he did. He was steady as an Irish stone, he was. Ma was so impressed, she cried.

Ma had bedded Emmet down in front of the hearth and

wrapped him in the cotton bedspread that she and Da used.
She made Muc lie on his other side. The most important thing,
she said, was to get him warm again. He had stumbled in all
confused, his breath slow and shallow. She couldn't even feel a
beat in his chest. By the time I got there with the jumper full
of eggs, Emmet was already asleep, but it was a fitful sleep. I
sat beside him at the hearth, deathly cold myself. I'd walked
extra slow with that clumsy, clumsy jumper so full of eggs; it
took me twice as long to get home as it had to go out to the
woods. I rubbed at my feet and then my hands and then my
feet again, till the feeling finally came back, all painful at first,
like fir needles pricking hard. Much longer outside and I would
have gotten frostbite, for sure. But I knew I wasn't bad off anything like what Emmet must have been feeling. Little Paddy
nestled against me and we watched Emmet's cheeks flame red
and his nose run yellow, while Ma hurried down to his hut to
get his ma, pushing her way through what had turned into a
true blizzard.

Emmet and his ma stayed with us overnight because everyone was afraid to move him home in this weather. His ma sat
with his head on her lap and stroked his hair. All night long he
alternated between sweating with fever and crying out from
the aches of chill. I knew, because I woke often through the
night and watched from the shadows.

I should have fought with him when he took off his jumper.
I probably couldn't have prevailed—who ever prevailed with
Emmet?—but I hadn't even tried. And I should have fought
more with Miss Susanna. I should have insisted. But I didn't

take the time. The truth was, I wanted to get those eggs home to little Paddy fast. Not just little Paddy, of course—we had to share them fairly with everyone. But it was little Paddy who was most on my mind. So I had let Emmet sacrifice himself and I had backed away from a brawl with Miss Susanna. It was as simple and ugly as that. I kept doing bad things. Something was wrong with my soul.

Then this morning Emmet vomited. Many times. At first it was a stinking green puddle. Then only spit. Then dry heaves. Finally, it seemed his stomach was calm. It was midafternoon now, and he lay there breathing fast and shallow, his eyes all glittery, his lips crusted white, and still he insisted on having some of the egg mix.

Ma was equally insistent that Emmet's ma should have a break from tending to him. "Move along," she said to Emmet's ma again. "Go sit with the rest of your family. Let Lorraine tend to Emmet for a bit."

Emmet's ma shook her head, but heavily. Lack of sleep weighed her down.

Ma pulled her to her feet. "Go on, I said."

"Slow now," Emmet's ma whispered to me as I took her place. "Feed him slow."

I knew that, of course. The last thing I wanted was for Emmet to vomit again. None of us could afford to lose food that way. He'd kept down the water his ma had dribbled into his mouth so far today—and that was good, at least. But eggs were different from water.

I watched his ma pick her way around people and settle

against Emmet's da's chest. Alana had her ma's cup full and ready for her. She handed it over. They touched foreheads for a moment as the cup changed hands. A long moment. And though Alana was only fourteen, she seemed like a full-grown woman right then—aching with a full-grown woman's concerns.

Kearney was busy eating his egg and turnips, but Kyla watched her ma and her big sister and she wiggled in closer to them. They were scared. Petrified.

So was I. No one had said the word *pneumonia* yet, but I knew the signs. We all did. Carrick had had pneumonia last winter. It took him weeks and weeks to recover, and when he did, we all said it was a miracle. So we knew about pneumonia. We knew about what was ailing Emmet. Pneumonia often came after a person got so very, very cold.

Unless it was tuberculosis.

I hadn't ever seen anyone with tuberculosis. You weren't allowed to go near them. But I knew many times people thought they had pneumonia and then it turned out to be tuberculosis. We hadn't had that disease on this farm. But other farms had had it. I remembered the row of fresh burial mounds in the graveyard that Sunday in mid-December when we kids had our first giving.

My shoulders spasmed hard. Good, that shook off the morbid image. Emmet couldn't have tuberculosis. Ma wouldn't have let all the others come into our cottage if she suspected he did. Ma was careful and cunning.

"What you waiting for?" croaked Emmet. "That egg's not

going to fly into my mouth on its own. Are you afraid I'll bite you?"

Such a stream of words. I'd thought he wasn't able to say hardly anything. I tried to keep the shock off my face. "Of course not."

"Really? I dare you to feed me with your fingers."

I took a pinch of egg and held it to his mouth.

"I was joking. You probably shouldn't touch my mouth."

I stuffed the egg between his teeth.

He seemed to squash it around with his tongue a while. The lump in his skinny throat moved up and down again as he swallowed. He looked at me and lifted his eyebrows. "So you're a brave idiot too."

"I'm trying to be."

"You were already half there to start with." He gave a wavery smile.

"Another bad joke deserves another pinch of egg." I stuffed it into his mouth with a forced grin.

He took longer to swallow it this time. "I think I should wait. A bit of an experiment this is, you see."

"It is that." I hadn't eaten my egg yet and the smell of Emmet's egg was so hard to ignore. Plus I knew it would taste best hot. "Would you mind if I ate while you wait?"

He closed his eyes. That seemed pretty much to be an answer I could take any way I pleased. I smoothed his hair away from his cheeks. He was hot to the touch.

I ate my eggs and turnip. Even though we'd get this only every other day, it seemed fantastically luxurious. Like in a fairy tale. I looked at the silent eaters all around the room. This was surely lifting spirits, but would it really be enough to bring back their strength?

Alana caught my eye. She came over and sat by me. "When he wakes, I'll feed him next."

I flinched, as though I'd been slapped. Or, worse, robbed. But I nodded. She was his big sister, after all. And she was older than me.

"Do you wonder about them?"

"Who?" I asked.

"Fiona's family."

"Nearly all the time. I bet their ma rationed out the hard-boiled eggs so that they all have something in their bellies when they arrive in Galways."

"You know she did," said Alana. "And they might have arrived already—yesterday if everything went right. But even if they had troubles, they'll arrive by the end of today."

"Fiona and Iona and Murray and Neil and Corey and little Aeden. It's funny to think of them in a big city."

"Not just them. Margaret, too. Your dear Margaret." Alana squeezed my hand.

I'd been trying not to think of Margaret. "Too bad we couldn't have had this meal before they left. They would have enjoyed it."

"Tomorrow they'll get on the ship and once they arrive in Glasgow they'll have plenty of eggs to eat."

"Are you sure?"

"Almost. My da and ma have been talking, mulling it over.

Da's changed his mind. He says emigrating is a good thing now. Life will be better for Fiona's family in Scotland."

"I hope so."

"Da says we should go to America."

My breath caught like a spike in my chest. I looked at Emmet's sleeping face and shook my head. "But your da was the one who said the ships themselves were coffins."

"Those are the ships to Canada—like Fiona's da said. There are other ships. Some go to South America, but Da says we'd never take one of them because they advise you to bring a gun to fight off criminals. Imagine that—moving to someplace where people need guns to defend themselves."

I didn't want to imagine it. I stared at her.

"Anyway, some ships go directly to the United States—not Canada. They come over to England carrying cotton, then they leave from Liverpool and go back to a big city called New Orleans. It's in the south of the United States. Where it's warm all year round. People love it there."

"Cotton ships? But that means they aren't made for carrying people, so they're just like the Canadian timber ships. Like what Fiona's da said. They'll be just as awful."

"Da doesn't think so. He says when Emmet gets well, we're going, like Fiona's family."

I couldn't bear the thought of Emmet going. But he wouldn't go, really—this was just a dream of his da's. "And where will your da get the money for the tickets?" I asked as gently as I could manage. "It's only a few shillings to go to Scotland. But that journey's nothing—a day to get to Dublin and then a few hours from Dublin to Glasgow. Da told us. Going across the Atlantic Ocean is totally different. It takes six weeks. More, even. And they say going to America costs even more than going to Canada. It must cost a fortune."

"It doesn't." Alana shook her head. "The cotton ships need weight going back. You see, the ocean can get rough, especially in winter, so ballast is important."

"Ballast?"

"The Irish passengers. They're ballast—they keep the ships from turning over. The cotton companies want Irish passengers. Da says he'll find the money. And some of the landlords are even talking about paying the tickets themselves, just to keep people from dying on their land."

"Is that the truth?"

"It's what Da heard. Anyway, we'll find the money for the tickets. And Da says the most important thing is keeping us alive. Your plan of stealing eggs won't do that."

"We don't steal. And it isn't just my plan."

"However you get them, eggs alone won't put flesh on you. That's what Ma says."

"Eggs are better than nothing," I said.

"Really? Look what happened to Emmet."

I winced.

"I shouldn't have said that." Alana put her hand on my arm.

"No. You're right," I managed to mumble.

Alana turned her head away. "We're just scared. Emmet's so sick. But I'm sorry I said that, Lorraine."

Emmet coughed right then, as if on cue, and rolled onto his

side. Phlegm drooled out his mouth. It was tinged with blood.

I stood up. I didn't know what to do. Emmet had to get better. The eggs had to keep coming. Life had to go on. *No more deaths, please, oh, please.* "I'm sorry too. So sorry."

I handed Emmet's cup of egg and turnip to Alana, and I went over to join the circle that had formed around little Paddy. Pointy was in the center, pecking at a dried-out cabbage leaf. His bottom was all dirty from diarrhea. The chick was hungry, and greens, fresh or dry, weren't right. He needed meal. But the children didn't know that. Noreen and Sheelagh and Carrick and Kearney were all laughing. It was amazing how a bit of egg in your belly and the sight of a fluffy chick, even with a dirty bottom, could change your world for a moment. It was snowing outside hard as the day before. The winds whipped around the corners of our cottage with a shriek. And Emmet lay there in fevered sleep coughing up brown-red mucus. Yet they could laugh. And they were right. What was the point of not laughing? The egg and turnip was delicious. The chick was darling, even in his desperation. Those children should seize every moment of pleasure they could. There were so few.

I squeezed my eyes shut to hold in whatever wanted to come out.

CHAPTER NINETEEN

Meal

Y ou can't go out in this weather, Lorraine." Ma stood by the door, blocking it. It was a pathetic gesture. She looked like I could topple her with a light push. She'd stayed up much of the night, sitting on a stool with her face to the fire and her back to the room, sewing.

I looked over at Emmet's ma. She was wiping Emmet's forehead with a wet rag. He was groaning in feverish sleep. Another exhausted woman, her face held nothing—not worry, not anger, not even fear—she was so shattered. She didn't look at me.

I looked over at little Paddy. He was lying on his belly, propped up on his elbows, watching Pointy peck at the dirt floor. He was as thin as ever. He had stopped eating his gruel, so all he ever ate was eggs, which came only every other day, and buttermilk. His energy was still close to nothing. Only the antics of Pointy could make him perk up. But that chick was moving more erratically now. He was weak.

I looked back at Ma. "You know I have to."

Ma shook her head. "Da wouldn't allow it."

"Da's not here."

Ma blinked and pursed her lips. "You'll lose your way. It's like trying to see gray against gray out there, the air is so thick."

"I'll manage."

"She won't even be there," whispered Ma. "Who's going into town in this weather?"

"Da. That's where he went, right?"

"But only because the weather is such a hardship, someone might pay him a halfpenny for doing a chore or an errand. No one who can avoid it is going outside today."

Ma might be right. Miss Susanna would probably curl in front of her hearth today rather than ask her da to take her to town. And even if she did ask, her da would be gone in the head to agree. But what if she did ask—and what if he did agree? As far as I could see, Miss Susanna got her way on everything. Her da might be the only person she had in the world, but she might be the only person he had too. He gave her everything. Or that's what it seemed like to me.

"I have to be at the graveyard at noon. That's all there is to it, Ma. I have to try."

"We have enough eggs for days and days to come."

"It's not just eggs," I said, so quietly I was sure little Paddy couldn't hear. "It's meal for Pointy."

Ma's face went slack. "Paddy loves that chick."

"So please move aside."

"You can't go with bare feet, Lorraine. It was Emmet's bare feet as much as his bare chest that got him so cold, and that's what made him so weak the sickness could grab him. Your uncle Odran was right about shoes."

I held up the rags in my hands. "I'll tie these around my feet."

"Come here, my daughter." Ma went to her sewing basket.

She took out three pairs of hide shoes. Small ones from the stoat pelt and two bigger ones from hare pelts. On all of them she'd sewn the Celtic trinity knot, made from a thin strip of hide. "I was hoping you and Paddy and Emmet could wear these playing outside soon." She pursed her lips. "But today it'll only be you. My daughter. My cunning and brave daughter."

I put on the smaller of the two hare pairs. "Thank you, Ma. I love them."

"Let's wrap those rags around your legs." Ma was already kneeling, wrapping one leg. I wrapped the other.

I kissed her on top of the head. Then I slipped outside, shutting the door fast behind me. The wind stole my breath in an instant. Ma was wrong about the color—the air that had been gray earlier was now white. But she'd been right about the difficulty—the boreens were impossible to find in the clouds of snow dust. That was just as well; I trudged in as straight a line as I could manage out to the road into town. A straight line meant a shorter path, after all.

The road was a bumpy mess of frozen ruts made by the wheels of carts and deep holes made by the hooves of horses. I fell repeatedly. It was just a mile and a half, but by the time I got to the graveyard, I was a mess of icy mud slop.

I waited for the bells of the Protestant church to ring at noon. I waited dutifully. They never did. And I knew I had arrived there well before the appointed time—the sun in the sky told me as much. Was the rector ill? Was he so hungry he'd forgotten?

Such a huge sky. It was three shades of blue—kind of sea colored near the horizon, then more milky, then bright and clear and true blue. Granny always said Ireland was made of every shade of green imaginable. But today Ireland was blue on top and white on the bottom. I breathed in that clean cold air and felt I was breathing the whole sky into me, the whole world, to the tips of my fingers and toes, to the tips of the very hair on my head.

But I was here for a reason. Where oh where was she? I waited and waited. I could hear Ma in my head: Miss Susanna stayed home today, like any sensible person. *Let Ma's voice be wrong.*

Most of the time that I was waiting, the road was empty in both directions as far as I could see. Now and then someone passed, and gave me a quick, suspicious glance, but hurried on their way, bent into the wind or against it—but always bent. I stepped from foot to foot to keep my limbs alive. It was now snowing yet again. The wind had brought in new clouds that simply dumped everywhere. Yet somehow that snow felt warmer. It seemed to smother the wind. I imagined the sea foam all calm now. Ah, I could wait a while longer if the wind would stay hushed like this. After all, Miss Susanna wasn't like anyone else. She might well not do the sensible thing.

A horse-drawn, four-wheel cart approached on Bridge Street. It had two drivers on the front seat, one holding the reins and the other holding a rifle. Two soldiers in uniforms walked alongside the cart, also holding rifles. I figured they were on the way to the workhouse.

Within moments men and boys appeared. They came from doors that shut behind them quickly. They came from around the corner of buildings and from behind me in the graveyard and down from balconies. They came from everywhere. Maybe twenty of them. Maybe more. Most were dressed in rags. Most had no hat. Most had no shoes. They walked toward the cart.

The soldiers shouted for the little crowd to halt.

But the crowd kept coming toward the cart. They held pitchforks or scythes with long handles. Some held rocks. Some carried big sticks. They didn't say anything. They didn't need to. The cart was piled high with giant cloth sacks, the kind that held wheat and oats.

I didn't know what a cart of grains was doing on Bridge Street in a January snowstorm—it couldn't be heading for the workhouse, that was for sure. Where had those grains been stored all season? Who had ordered them delivered now? I'd never know. But I had no doubt what those men and boys wanted.

Inside my head I cheered for them to succeed. They'd tilled the land. They'd harvested the crop. They had a right—a right to their own production, a right not to starve. Whoever that grain belonged to legally, morally it belonged to those men and boys.

But I couldn't take my eyes off those rifles. Pitchforks, scythes, rocks, sticks on one side. Rifles on the other.

And who was that? I couldn't see the front of him. But he was the right height. I couldn't see his jumper well because he had some kind of cloth draped across his shoulders and back, but it was a fisherman's jumper for sure—a jumper from the Aran Islands. No!

The soldiers aimed their rifles, but they aimed high. It was just a show. Of course. But it was enough. The men and boys would go away now, back to where they came from. Whoever they were; wherever they came from. They had to. They couldn't win, no matter how right they were. They'd leave now.

But they didn't.

And then the soldiers fired. Good Lord, they fired level!

I threw myself on the ground and crawled behind a gravestone. Gunshots continued. And shouts. And screams. And the neighing of horses. And more gunshots. I pushed my back against the gravestone and pulled my knees up to my chest and hid my face between my knees. *Let it stop. Please, please, let it stop.*

Then it did; the shots ended. I heard the horses moving again, the cart rolling in its clumpity way. Then nothing. I waited to be sure. Snow could be so very quiet, it could be deceptive. I waited until my bottom went numb. When I peeked out, I saw no one at first, but then I spied her: a woman kneeling over a body in the road.

If I went home the way I'd come, I'd have to pass them. I didn't want to pass them. I could get home without taking that road. Sure, I'd have to cut across private property, and people didn't take to trespassers. But I was just a girl. No one would be afraid of a girl crossing their property. No one would throw me in gaol for that.

I didn't want to pass the woman and the body.

But the body had on shoes. Thick-soled shoes.

A searing lump formed in my chest. I had to see that body. I walked out to the road.

The woman had pulled the body half onto her lap now. And it wasn't a dead body after all, it was talking. I came closer. The man's belly was covered in blood, but he was talking and crying. And I didn't recognize him—I didn't know him at all. Relief warmed me. But the woman was looking at me, and I mustn't show relief on my face; after all, a man had been shot. So I lowered my face fast.

And there in my path was a little pile of something yellowish brown, getting quickly covered by snow. I stopped and stooped and wiped off the snow. It was grain. I looked around to see if anyone else saw that pile.

"Go ahead," called the woman. "It fell out when they split a sack in half to carry it easier. Get it before the others come back."

I didn't ask who the others were. I didn't ask if I could help her somehow. I didn't really think. I just grabbed two fistfuls of grain and hurried away. But the faster I went, the more I stumbled. And I couldn't afford to fall, I couldn't afford to open my hands to break a fall and lose this meal. So I slowed down.

Everything was white, but I kept seeing the red on the man's belly. He was talking, though. He'd survive. He was talking.

The road seemed so long now. It was taking me forever to get to the point where I could turn off the road and head toward our farm. I expected the others, whoever they were, to appear at any moment. To yell "halt" at me, like the soldiers had yelled at the crowd. To make me empty my hands into a bowl. To haul me off to gaol. Stealing was bad—for stealing they'd imprison me for sure.

Where was that turnoff? Where where where? The wind had swept the surface of the snow level on both sides of the road, so I'd never be able to find my own tracks from when I'd come earlier. I was lost. And I was still seeing all that red.

By the time I finally decided to turn off the road, I was jumpy and half gone in the head. But I'd judged right somehow, because moments later I passed the cottiers' huts. Two of them were puffing out black smoke that reeked of peat from the hole in the roof—Alana's hut and Teagan's hut. One was cold, abandoned—Fiona's hut. And one was nothing but low humps, snow-covered ashes—Deirdre's hut.

I plowed through that snow as fast as I could now.

"Lorraine! Lorraine, is that you?"

I turned around. "Da!" I stood there till he caught up to me and I threw myself into his arms. "Oh, Da!"

"Where were you? You weren't in town, were you?"

I banged my forehead against his chest. "Oh, Da."

"What did you see?"

I kept banging my head.

"Tell me?"

"All that blood."

"Oh, Lorraine." He hugged me tighter.

"Were you there, Da? I thought I saw you."

"Your uncle Odran is right, Lorraine. It's time to stand and fight."

"But against rifles, Da?"

He hugged me tighter. "We won't talk about it. Agreed, Lorraine? It would only worry your ma to death."

I nodded.

Da pushed me out to arm's length. "Tell me you understand."

"I understand."

We walked the rest of the way in silence.

CHAPTER TWENTY

Shoes

Pointy didn't eat the grain, not even a pinch of it. I think he was just too weak to give it a try. He died the very night I brought that grain home. Right after we had our evening meal. We looked over and he was simply lying on his side, limp.

We said prayers over him. Then Ma wrapped him in a bit of cloth and handed him to Da to bury behind our cottage in the snow.

"I'm coming," said little Paddy.

"It's too cold, Paddy," said Da.

"I don't feel the cold."

"You'll get sick, Paddy," said Ma. "You saw what happened to Emmet from being out in the cold."

"I need to help bury Pointy."

"Come on, Paddy, you're a big boy. You understand."

"You're my ma. You understand."

Ma looked flustered.

"You can't," said Da. "And that's that."

"If you don't let me come," said little Paddy, "I will hate you. For the rest of my life."

We all stared at him. Little Paddy had never said anything

that bad ever. Even Emmet and his ma seemed shocked. They turned their heads away.

Little Paddy looked at Ma. "And I will hate you, too." He looked at me. "And I will hate you."

I took off my jumper and put it on little Paddy over his jumper. He'd shrunk so much, mine fit over his easily. I tied his new hide shoes on his feet. "I'll carry him," I said. "On my back. That's his favorite."

"No you won't, Lorraine." Da squatted in front of little Paddy. "Your sister and ma are staying inside because it's so cold. But I'll carry you outside to bury this chick if you apologize for saying that awful thing and if you promise never to say that again to any of us."

"I promise."

So Da and little Paddy buried Pointy.

The next night was an egg night, as we'd come to call them. Everyone gathered in our cottage and ate eggs with kale scrambled into them. Paddy ate only half his portion, little though it was. Emmet gobbled his own portion, then promptly vomited it all. But the rest of the kids seemed happy. Egg days felt like holidays to them, kind of like a party. Even the fact that Pointy had died couldn't keep them down; having something substantial to eat was that good.

The adults weren't festive, though. They argued about the merits of emigration. Da had a long list of questions. How would we find jobs in America? How would we find a home? Did foreigners have rights? What would happen if we got sick? Teagan's da said all those questions were the reason why we should trust in the Lord and stay in Ireland.

But Emmet's da seemed to have all the answers. There were jobs galore in America for those who knew how to farm. He'd heard all about it. And Irish stuck together in neighborhoods and helped one another. "I'm taking my family to America as soon as Emmet is strong enough to travel."

My hands curled so tight, my nails dug into my palms.

"As soon as I get together the money for the tickets," he added. The cost had turned out not to be as low as he'd originally thought.

My hands eased.

That night I heard Da talking with Ma about how much money he'd get for selling Muc and Bo Bo. How many tickets could he buy?

I was glad little Paddy had fallen asleep fast and didn't hear any of it. And I was glad Emmet and his ma were also asleep. I rolled over onto the dirt so that my body was pressed against Muc's and I whispered into her stiff back hairs, "Don't you listen, girl. We need you." Then I put my fingers in my ears and willed myself to sleep.

The day after that Ma made porridge from the grain meal that was supposed to be for Pointy. But little Paddy didn't eat it. He didn't cry. He hadn't cried at all after Pointy's death. He didn't even complain. He just said he wasn't hungry, then sat silent, not tasting the porridge, not even looking at it, until Ma finally allowed him to go lie on our sleeping mat, where he promptly fell asleep.

Emmet ate the porridge, though. And he kept it down.

His cheeks were less flushed and his eyes weren't glassy anymore. That night Ma convinced Emmet's ma to go back to her own hut. She promised we'd look after Emmet. She said he was on the mend, and if Emmet's ma didn't watch out, she'd wind up sick next from pure exhaustion. When Emmet's ma protested, Ma said, "If you're sick, how will you go to America?" So Emmet's ma left.

We were the five of us that night, our family plus Emmet. It felt better. I liked Emmet's ma, but our home felt right without her.

Everyone went to sleep early.

The next day was sunny, and though snow still covered the ground, it was warmer.

I looked around the room. Little Paddy lay on our sleeping mat because he was too wobbly to get up. Ma sat at his side singing softly. More a croon than a lullaby. I hated listening to it.

Da did too. A muscle in the side of his jaw kept twitching as he watched Ma and little Paddy from his place at the table. He crossed his arms over his chest and his fingers drummed on his arms. Finally, he gave me a stern look, and he stood up and walked over to Ma. "I'm going out."

"Please be back in time for the evening meal," said Ma. "Everyone's coming. Eggs again."

Da gave a little grunt of assent and left.

I just bet he was off to town.

I thought of the man with blood all over his belly.

It seemed that nothing good could ever happen.

At least Emmet had slept well. Now he sat by the fire and motioned me over.

"It's time," he whispered.

"Time?"

"I was hoping we could wait till I was well again. But we can't. Look at Paddy. He needs food. We have to do something now."

I nodded. "You mean with Miss Susanna again? I was thinking the same thing." In fact, though the egg supply was dwindling fast, that wasn't what was on my mind most. I'd been thinking that little Paddy needed a new pet. That was the only thing that seemed to make him eat, having a pet. Maybe Miss Susanna would think of a way to get that for him. "But I don't know how to contact Miss Susanna. There's no reason to hope she'll be waiting for us in the woods."

"You have to go straight up to the castle door."

"Are you gone in the head? She told me never to do that. Her da would go into a fury if he knew we were her friends."

"Don't tell him."

"Oh." I sidled closer to Emmet. Miss Susanna couldn't get cross if I didn't get her in trouble. "Yes, I could do that. If I only had an excuse for going to the castle."

"Right."

"But I have no excuse."

"Yes you do. Look under the table leg."

"What?"

"The one there. Closest to the hearth. Just shove it a little."

I got up and pushed on one corner of the table. It moved

slightly. And there on the floor where the leg had been a moment before was a crushed bit of red leather. I picked it up. Why, it was a dolly shoe. And I recognized it. The dolly Geraldine wore a long green dress, but I'd seen her feet peeking out from under it when she was seated on the cover at one of our parties. Her shoes were red. I quick tucked it inside my jumper and sat beside Emmet again.

"You stole it," I whispered.

"I took it," said Emmet.

"Isn't that the same thing?"

"Not if I intended to give it back."

"But why?"

"Don't you think that doll's dress is the color of shamrocks?"

"I do, now that you say it."

"She's an Irish doll in her soul."

I was trying to follow his logic. "I guess so."

"She was willing to lend us her shoe."

"To do what with?"

"Whatever we needed. And now we need it. It's an excuse. You can say you found it and you wondered if it belonged to anyone in the castle."

"I didn't find it."

"Sure you did. Under the table leg. But you don't have to say that."

"I won't say that."

"What will you say if they ask where you found it?"

"What should I say?" I asked.

"I don't know."

"Then I'll just stand silent. As though I'm too scared to talk."

"That might work."

I patted my jumper over the spot where the little red shoe was. "What if whoever answers the door just takes the shoe and shuts the door again?"

"They probably will. But Miss Susanna will know it was you. Who else would it have been?"

I nodded. "So she'll expect me in the woods." I pushed his shoulder gently. "Well done, Emmet. I'm so glad you're my partner."

"You're going to be afraid."

"I will not. The shoe is a good excuse."

"I meant the dogs."

I hadn't thought of the dogs, I didn't know why. They should have been the first thing on my mind. I pulled my legs in under me and rocked my body over them. "I'll look for a stick as I walk there. A big one."

"Bad idea. You might just make the dogs mad."

"So what do I do?"

"Stand still. If they come at you, just stand still."

"But I'll be all alone. I'd rather run."

"Dogs chase things that run."

"What if they bite me?"

"Maybe they won't."

I rubbed my hands together and rocked again. I imagined dog teeth. How tall would the dogs be? Would they bite my legs, or my arms, or my face? I suddenly hated them.

Emmet touched my arm. "I wish I could go with you."

"So do I. But you have your part to do." I reached for my hare-hide shoes, at the side of the hearth. They were lovely warm as I tied them onto my feet. Gratitude for them made me almost forget those hideous dogs. "I'm leaving without telling Ma." I gave Emmet another small push on the shoulder. "You have to explain to her good enough that she isn't cross when I get home. That's your part. Plus next time, you'll be the one to go and I'll stay home."

CHAPTER TWENTY-ONE

Fox

I stood in the little woods where Miss Susanna and I had met in the past and wondered about the best way to approach the castle. The last time I'd planned on going up to the door—on my visit to Miss Susanna—I'd headed for the rear, the door that was closest to the woods. I'd simply plucked up my courage and done it. But I didn't know then that one of the dogs' jobs was to guard the henhouse out rear of the castle. Dogs wouldn't be forgiving if I went near the henhouse. It was better to approach by the front door. That's where visitors usually came, I bet.

I walked in a big arc out to a small country road and followed it. This added a lot to the distance—maybe a half mile more than what it would have taken to go directly from the woods up to the house. Still, it was a good plan. I was cold by this point, very, but I had managed not to think about it so much. Now, though, I shivered. I wanted to run, to heat up. But Emmet said dogs chase things that run. So I counted slowly and made sure I took only one step for every count.

Every step closer I got, I expected to hear barks and snarls and then face sharp teeth. But there was nothing, no noise at all, as I passed through a stone wall and followed a path all the way up to the castle. The main door was tall enough for a giant to enter. It was painted blue, and in the center of it was a brass knocker in the shape of a fox. Foxes were wondrous creatures. Quiet and attentive. You couldn't see them unless they allowed you to. Meeting a fox felt like a good omen.

I would speak with Miss Susanna. And this time I'd make sure we had a plan that would work—a plan that would save us all.

Unless she wasn't home.

I stared at that fox. He was urging me on. Stand and fight.

I was grateful to the fox. Even if Miss Susanna wasn't home, I would speak with someone. I would make them understand. I could do this.

I tried to lift the knocker by the fox's front feet, but it wouldn't budge. Finally I figured out that only the head moved. I lifted it as high as it would go and let it fall. *Bang.* I jumped back. The loudness had surprised me. It felt rude. I didn't want to appear rude. Firm, but not rude. I tried to smile at whoever would open the door.

Nothing happened. No one came.

There was no choice. I lifted the knocker and let it fall again. *Bang.*

Barks came from within. Lots of them. Deep and loud.

I prepared to die.

The door opened.

An overweight woman wearing a black dress and a white apron stood with a giant dog on either side of her and a third one behind her. Irish wolfhounds. I almost laughed. I knew stories about Irish wolfhounds. Everyone did. They used to be a common dog in Ireland, but these days only the English had them. They were huge, the biggest dogs in the world people said, but they were also sweet-tempered. And these were sleek and well-fed, nothing like the snargling, rangy dogs that ran in packs through town. I nearly collapsed, I was so relieved.

"So now they're sending their children begging, are they?" said the woman. "That's the very worst. Listen, girl. We don't give food. Think about it. What would that do to your self-respect if you simply had things given to you all the time? I told the men. I told the women. What do you think workhouses are for? Go away now." She shut the door.

I stood there a moment, stunned. Slowly, slowly anger churned inside me. Self-respect? Workhouses?

I banged the knocker again.

When the door opened, I was standing with my hand out-stretched and the red shoe in my palm.

"I told you . . . What's this?" The woman picked up the shoe between thumb and pointer. "Where did you get this?"

I just looked at her.

"I asked you a question."

I swallowed. Words wouldn't come.

"Wait right here." She shut the door.

Minutes later it opened again. The woman stood there and Miss Susanna stood beside her, her face pinched in worry. The woman held the shoe, still between thumb and pointer finger.

"This is my doll's shoe," said Miss Susanna at last. "Mrs. Cothran wants to know how you got it."

I blinked.

"Can't you talk?" asked Mrs. Cothran.

What a good idea. I shook my head. Then I mimicked searching around and picking something up from the ground.

"She found my doll's shoe," said Miss Susanna. She laughed. "How nice. That was nice of her, Mrs. Cothran, don't you think?"

"I think she shouldn't have been walking around the property."

"Well, you don't know that she was. I might have lost it in town."

"Then how would she have known to bring it here?"

"Maybe she's cunning."

"Like a fox."

Like a fox. That was me. *Please let that be me.*

"Maybe she's looking for a handout." Mrs. Cothran gave a loud sniff. "Thank her and send her on her way."

"But it's cold out, Mrs. Cothran. She came from far away. Can't we let her come in and warm up first?"

"How do you know where she came from?"

"No one lives close, so visitors all come from far away. Please let's invite her in to warm up."

"Hmmm. Your father would never approve."

"I won't tell if you won't tell."

"It's not just me. What would Mrs. Addicott say?"

"I'll stay with her in the front room. Mrs. Addicott has no reason to go in there. She practically lives in the kitchen. And look how thin this girl is. She's shivering."

"I don't know."

"Dad won't be home till late. That's what he said. Please, Mrs. Cothran."

"I can't see that it would be much fun to spend time with a mute girl who knows nothing of the world."

"Would you rather I be alone all the time?"

Mrs. Cothran made a little circle of her mouth. "This once, Miss Susanna." She stepped aside.

"Well, come in already," ordered Miss Susanna.

I stepped into the entranceway onto a polished wood floor, and Miss Susanna shut the door behind me.

A dog licked right up my face, one big slurp. I backed against a wall.

"Go away, Donal," said Miss Susanna. She pointed to another room. "Go, all of you." She stamped her foot.

The three dogs trotted off.

Mrs. Cothran went into a different room and Miss Susanna followed her, so I followed Miss Susanna. The ceiling was high and the long room was cold and drafty. There were windows along the outer wall and bookshelves along the parallel inner wall. At the other end of the room was a hearth where embers smoldered. Mrs. Cothran added wood from the pile beside the hearth, till a fire crackled and burned bright, and the room began to heat.

"Thank you, Mrs. Cothran. You can go away now too."

"I don't know about that. We don't know if the girl's trust-worthy, after all."

"She brought me the shoe," said Miss Susanna. "That's trustworthy enough for me."

Mrs. Cothran sighed. She looked me up and down and sighed again. Then she left.

"Sit on the sofa," said Miss Susanna.

I looked around. Sofa?

Miss Susanna frowned. "You don't have to keep playing dumb." She sat on a long, plumpy thing in front of the hearth. "Come sit beside me."

I did.

"How did you get Geraldine's shoe?"

"Emmet took it."

"So he's rotten, to use his own word."

"Not at all. He figured it would come in handy somehow. And it did. You didn't come to the graveyard."

"Did you go?"

"I waited for you a long time."

"But it was snowing. You're such an idiot, Lorraine."

"I keep my word."

Miss Susanna made an ugly face.

"What happened when you visited the other castle?" I asked.

"They wouldn't let me wander around outside on my own. They said there were too many beggars and thieves. And too many wild dogs."

"Your dogs aren't scary, by the way."

"I know."

"You made me and Emmet think they were."

"Well . . ." She shrugged. "If the dogs came across you outside, they'd bark like mad even as they licked you, so they would have given you away, and that would have ruined us."

"Hmmm. So is that the end of things?" I said. "You couldn't find anything at the other castle, so that's the end of your plan."

"I can come up with another plan."

"How?"

"I always figure things out."

How thick Miss Susanna could be. "Everything will have gone wrong by the time you do."

"What do you mean?"

"The cottiers are talking about leaving for America." I wouldn't say Da was talking about it too. The words would taste too bad.

"That's a good idea," said Miss Susanna.

No, it wasn't. But Miss Susanna would never understand. She didn't know Ireland, not really. She'd never know Ireland. She'd never ever guess at how precious this country was. "It costs a lot for tickets."

"Well."

"'Well'—do you realize that 'well' is your answer to everything? I hate that word."

"Don't be mad at me. It's not my fault."

"Isn't it?"

"Don't be daft."

I felt like a giant hole was opening up below, ready to swallow me whole. "Everything is going wrong, and there's nothing to be done about it. Is that it?"

"Not everything is going wrong. Think of Susanna."

"What?"

"The cute little chick."

"The chick died."

"Oh no!" Miss Susanna took my hand. Then her eyes widened. "Did . . . did anyone else die?"

I shook my head. "But Emmet caught pneumonia."

"I keep thinking it can't be as bad as you say . . . but the chick died . . . it really died . . . and Emmet . . . well . . . I'll figure out another plan, Lorraine. I promise. Wait here." Miss Susanna left the room.

I stared at the fire. It was true, it wasn't her fault. How could any of this be the fault of one English girl? And even promising to do something when she couldn't do anything—that wasn't her fault either. She meant well. All this rage I felt, it didn't belong anywhere. No one controlled the murrain. The spuds failed . . . that's all there was to it . . . the spuds failed. And no one controlled the weather. It was simply a perishing winter— colder than we'd ever had it before. No one was to blame.

Only something felt very wrong. Lots of things felt very wrong. Four-wheeled carts piled high with grains that rolled through a town where people were starving felt as wrong as anything could be.

"Here." Miss Susanna hurried back and held out a folded blanket. "Sleep under it. Don't get pneumonia."

What a funny girl. A few dozen eggs. A blanket. And she

thought she could fix the world. No one could fix anything. Not right now—not in Ireland. And there was no point asking her to find little Paddy a new pet. There was no point to anything. My head filled with noise. "Thank you. I'm going home now."

She didn't offer me anything to eat. I was surprised. But I wouldn't have accepted anyway. I couldn't think straight with all the noise in my head.

I left by the front door. I walked down the path, through the gate in the stone wall, out to the country road. I walked and walked.

A man on horseback came up the road toward me. I moved to the side.

He passed me, then turned around and came back. "What are you doing with that blanket?"

I looked up at him and the irritation in his voice somehow changed me; for a moment the noise in my head paused. "I'm hoping to stop anyone else from getting pneumonia."

The man got off his horse. "Stop walking."

I stopped.

"Where did you get that blanket?"

"Are you Miss Susanna's father?"

"How do you know my daughter's name?"

There came that churn in my belly again—the smallest rebirth of anger. "You should ask her that."

"And those shoes. They look like they're from a freshly killed hare. Did you kill a hare on my property?"

I didn't know. I wasn't sure anymore whether these shoes were from the hare I'd killed or from one of those Uncle Odran had brought us. But maybe Uncle Odran's were killed on this land too. "Probably," I said, with a force that surprised me.

"You have no right to hunt here."

I lifted my chin, like Miss Susanna always did. "How does hunting hares hurt you, if you don't hunt them yourself?"

"What impertinence! You have no right to be on this land at all."

"This is a public road, and I'm part of the public. Besides, my father is one of your tenant farmers. So we pay rent to be here."

"Which farmer?"

"Does it matter? We are all starving. And freezing."

"Such exaggeration."

"How many have to die before you'll understand? Or maybe you'll never understand, all pampered in your castle." Emmet had used that word: *pampered*. Emmet had a way with words. I could honor him by mimicking him. It was important to honor those who deserved it. I walked again. Then I stopped and looked over my shoulder. He was watching me still, his face immobile. "Miss Susanna tries to be kind," I called back. "She'd like to fix things. She still believes people have the power to fix things. Isn't that too bad?" I walked home.

Part 5

Spring Comes,
1847

CHAPTER TWENTY-TWO

Ships

M a and I scrubbed rags. We scrubbed and scrubbed till they were white as snow. The snow had melted away weeks ago, but that white stayed before my eyes, so I knew these rags were snow white. Then we sewed. We made a perfect shirt and a perfect pair of breeches for little Paddy. And we made a perfect shroud.

We dressed little Paddy and wrapped him tight.

Good-bye, *dearthair beag*—little brother. With the final twist of the shroud, his face was gone.

Da dug his grave. He did it alone, though others wanted to help. He needed to do it alone. He made it very deep. I could have stood in that grave and been entirely underground.

The priest didn't come. He was busy all the time, going from one burial to the next; there were just too many for him to attend them all. Like Uncle Odran had said about the priest in Dublin. The word was that people were dying in droves all over Ireland. And I knew it was true. Last week I saw a line of bodies on the strand. Twenty-eight of them. They'd died as they were being carried to the hospital. People were arguing about where to bury them. It had to happen fast, for the risk of dogs attacking and disease spreading terrified everyone. And the hospital itself was scheduled to close. It couldn't handle all the sick, so it was simply going to close. Doctors were exhausted. Priests were exhausted. And both doctors and priests had died.

But Teagan's da knew the right words to say, so we all stood around little Paddy's body and listened. Then we prayed together. "May God hold you in the hollow of His hand," we said, over and over, till I felt those huge hands, till I was rolling in them myself. The words became a chant, and the chant was almost a comfort. Little Paddy would have joined in heartily. My *dearthàir beag* had loved chanting.

Once little Paddy was lowered into the ground, Emmet and his father shoveled the dirt back over him. Da watched, but he couldn't move.

Da and Ma and me. None of us touched one another. The others hugged us and cried and they left. But we stayed separate. Da and Ma and me. We went inside and lay down, each of us alone and cold. Maybe because it would feel disloyal to little Paddy to have the relief of touch when he could never have it again. Maybe just because we were spent.

The next day Ma and I washed little Paddy's jumper and his old raggedy shirt and breeches, and Teagan's ma took them to the workhouse, because neither Teagan's family nor Emmet's had anyone small enough for those clothes.

His shoes, though, they were given to Kearney. Ma had made them large enough to grow into, so they fit Kearney just right.

Kearney said, "Thank you." He said, "Next year, if we have a festival on Saint Brigid's Day, I'll be in the parade with my shoes."

We hadn't had a festival on Saint Brigid's Day this year.

And I felt almost sure Kearney would have long outgrown those shoes by the time we ever had a festival again.

And that same day, just one day after little Paddy went into the ground, the steward came around. With an announcement. There would be soup kitchens opening up in town for anyone in need. The government had decided that. The landlord thought it was a pity that anyone should come to depend on government like that, to be reduced to helplessness, but it wasn't up to him.

And that steward came with something else, too: an envelope. The landlord had decided, all on his own, to pay for tickets to America for any of his tenant farmers who wanted them. This wasn't a handout, he insisted. It was very different from what the government was doing. Rather, people could think of it as a final payment from their boss as they got started in the New World. Plus it served him, for he absolutely wouldn't allow deaths on his land. No disease. No burials. His property must remain untainted. It wasn't his fault that the Lord had seen fit to ruin the potato crop—he wanted no doubt about that. But he couldn't stand by and do nothing if terrible things were about to happen right here on his soil, given that anything planted this spring couldn't be harvested till fall. So off to America with anyone who wanted to go.

It was happening just like Emmet's da had said it would.

Da was allowed four tickets, since the steward's log book showed he had two children and a wife. Da held out his hand. I didn't even blink. I wasn't sure I had a heart to break anymore.

The steward didn't know about the deep, deep grave behind

our cottage. He didn't know about the graves behind the burned-down cottier hut, either. But as it turned out, that didn't matter, because the cottier families were not being offered ship tickets. Emmet's da was wrong about that part. The cottiers paid no rent; they had no right to the land. Unless they were healthy and strong, they were to leave immediately. Get off the land. It didn't matter where they went, just as long as they didn't die on the landlord's property. The steward would come around next week to check that all cottier huts were either full of strong people or empty and destroyed.

That night was an egg night. We still had them every other day, because Emmet and I went once a week to collect eggs in the wall behind the henhouse. The dogs came bounding out at us most of the time, but we just scratched them hard behind the ears and they licked us half to death and then they ran off to torment some hapless hare or red squirrel.

Miss Susanna never came out to greet us. I didn't know why, but I didn't go up and bang that fox knocker ever again. After all, if Miss Susanna had come up with a plan, she would have come out to us, all proud of herself. That wasn't a totally fair thing to think, I knew. She would have been full of energy, too, ready to help. She was good inside, maybe in spite of herself. And she kept us alive, I had to admit that. Those eggs were essential.

After a while I suspected she had left. I remembered she'd once told me she wouldn't be here in spring. So she was probably back in England. Maybe she'd left right after I last saw her in January; who knew? I didn't even know where in England she might have returned to. I didn't know much about Miss Susanna. She never mentioned family other than her da. She once said she played with two girls, but she didn't call them friends. We were the only ones she called friends.

So we went unbidden to that wall, Emmet and me. But no one shooed us away. That couldn't be an accident. Not with the dogs announcing our presence and bouncing around us as we gathered eggs. Maybe other people in that castle were good inside in spite of themselves too.

It was early, early spring. Or not even true spring yet—not according to the calendar. Saint Patrick's Day was coming the following week. There was talk that the seas were calming, that the crossing to America was less harsh now. So I expected the talk after our egg dinner to turn to emigration precisely when it did.

"What's the date of that ship you're traveling on?" asked Emmet's da.

"We've been talking about that," said Da. "Catherine and I have been talking."

"I bet you have. We need to get on a ship too. Lord, how I've been trying to scrape together the money for those tickets. I have to do it fast, before they drag us from our huts."

"We're not being dragged anywhere," said Teagan's da. "The workhouse here has closed its doors. They're being vicious. Last week a boy was thrown out for missing work because he attended his father's burial. Clifden has gone mad. But there are better places. We're walking to Galways and moving into the workhouse there. And we're waiting."

"Waiting for what?" said Da.

"It isn't just this landlord who's paying for people to go to America. They say the government is going to start emptying out the workhouses soon. Turns out shipping a family to North America costs less than supporting them in a workhouse for a year. So we'll wait. And when the workhouses are empty, we'll be among the few left, and we can find work. Maybe even on a farm again."

"If that's really true," said Emmet's da, "we'll walk with you to Galways. We won't wait for jobs, though. We'll leave on the first ship they put us on."

"I'll walk in my new shoes," said Kearney.

"You don't have to go live in the workhouse in Galways," said Da. "You can have our four tickets. That leaves you only two more to pay for, and you've got the money for that, right?"

I had been leaning against the wall, listening with a sense of doom. But now I sat up tall.

"What are you talking about?" said Emmet's da.

"We're staying here," said Da.

"We won't leave him, you see," said Ma.

I stood up and walked over to Ma and sat down and held her hand. No, we wouldn't leave little Paddy. Never. The world might be upside down, but at least this one thing would stay right. And not just this one thing. No—much more.

"Ireland is ours," I said in as steady a voice as I could manage. "It's Granny's and Paddy's and Ma's and Da's and Uncle Odran's and mine."

"That it is. Ireland will always be in our hearts too. You

take care of her for us, do that." Emmet's da gave me a quick nod. "I'm sorry for your loss, Francis, Catherine, Lorraine. I'm so sorry. And I thank you from the bottom of my heart."

Emmet stood up. "I'm not going with you." His voice was soft, but we could all hear it clearly.

Emmet's ma cried out. "What are you saying?"

Emmet looked at Da. "I can help you. I'm good at working in the fields. And this is my land too. I love Ireland. Will you let me live with you?"

"You don't understand, son," said Emmet's da. "America has promise. You could go to school."

"I could go to school here, if school was what I wanted."

"And what would you do in the maths here, son? Spend all your time counting up the dead around you? Emmet, my boy, if you think it's bad now, you have no idea of what's coming. It's going to get worse. Far worse. And no one knows when it'll get better again."

I waited for Emmet to say it—to say he'd never die anyplace but Ireland. But he didn't. He just looked at Da. His question hung in the air, and no matter how many words Emmet's da said, it wouldn't go away.

Da looked at Emmet's da.

Emmet's da dropped his head.

Emmet's ma cried. And Ma cried too. Losing a child was too hard. Damnably hard.

CHAPTER TWENTY-THREE

Sipping at the World

D a waited till April to go up to the landlord's house to get the seeds to sow. That was a few weeks later than usual, but winter had been so harsh, the earth was coming into spring late. Da had to borrow a handcart to carry those seeds back. I never learned how he explained what he'd done with the four ship tickets. But it seemed the landlord had had no idea of how he was going to find new tenant farmers for this year's crops, so maybe he was glad enough of Da's presence to experience strategic amnesia, as Uncle Odran would have said.

So there they were, Da and Emmet, plowing the grain fields. And here we were, Ma and me, tilling the soil of the kitchen garden. We planted those little buds we'd gouged out of the few spuds last autumn. And we had a few haws—pitiful few, but precious few—that Emmet's family and Teagan's family had managed to save. It only took one day to plant the whole garden.

Da and Emmet came home dirty and exhausted. But after a dinner of cabbage gruel and poached eggs, Emmet said, "I have something to show you."

I turned to Ma. "There will still be light for a while." It was true; the days were already getting longer.

Ma waved us out the door.

Emmet led me halfway up the hill that we climbed every time we gathered eggs. Then he veered off the path and squatted. I followed and squatted beside him, in the middle of dozens and dozens of tiny yellow flowers—cowslips, the first I'd seen this season. He broke off the top of one just where the skirts of the flower began and handed it to me, then he broke off the top of a second. We sucked out the nectar at the same time.

"It's grand," said Emmet, "sipping at the world like this."

"In July, I'll take you to a patch of fuchsia," I said. "Fuchsia nectar is even better."

"Promises, promises," he said. "You can't best me with a promise."

"Ah, so it's a competition, is it? Well, then, come with me." I headed to the path and ran up that hill, then over a ways, on the branch that Da and I took when we went to cut peat. I stopped at the very crest. "Look!"

"The Aran Islands," said Emmet. "I've seen them from a hillcrest before. And at night. They stood out against the silver of the sea."

"Not just the islands," I said. "Look that way. See? Can you see the spray? Those are the Cliffs of Moher."

We both leaned and stared and, what do you know, there they were, all gray and white, the majestic cliffs. I was seeing them at last. I laughed.

"You won," said Emmet. He crossed his arms at his chest and gave a deep, satisfied sigh. "Today, as we were plowing, the steward came by."

I shuddered. "Awful man."

"He had some things to say about Ireland. I wish you'd been there to hear. He called it 'bleak and rocky.' Can you imagine?"

"No one ever said he was anything but thick," I said. "Are you a good singer, Emmet?"

"Not in Alana's eyes. She says I'm terrible."

"I'm terrible too. Want to sing as we go back down the hill?"

"No. I want to be silent."

"That's not very friendly."

"It will be if we catch a hare."

"We don't have hunting rights, Emmet."

"So you think." He lifted his eyebrows. "The steward said something interesting today. He looked at my shoes and he said he had a message from the landlord for me."

"How could the landlord have sent you a message?"

"It wasn't for me exactly. It was for any tenant farmer's children wearing shoes made of hare hide. He said, 'Hunting hares doesn't hurt the landlord, because he doesn't hunt them himself.'" Emmet rubbed the side of his nose. "Seems pretty clear to me."

My cheeks had gone warm. "I agree." I pushed his shoulder. "You know, sometimes I think about Miss Susanna and I miss her."

"No one ever said you were anything but thick either." He laughed. But I knew he was thinking the same thing I was thinking: how lucky we were to have met her.

And so we walked down the hill silent as mice. But we

didn't see a hare. Nor a stoat. We didn't even see a songbird.

But, oh, there went a bat. The first bat I'd seen this spring. I thought of the blue underwing moth that had landed on little Paddy that day last August. The moth was the size of that bat. My breath came sad and heavy.

Emmet never talked about his ma and da. He never talked about Alana and Kyla and Kearney. But I knew he thought about them. I knew he was hoping for a letter. I knew he wondered where they were.

At least I'd always know where little Paddy was.

When we reached the bottom of the hill, I sang. Emmet joined me on the second word.

"May the road rise to meet you.
May the wind be always at your back.
May the sun shine warm upon your face,
The rains fall soft upon your fields.
And until we meet again,
May God hold you in the hollow of His hand."

POSTSCRIPT

In the early nineteenth century, Ireland was mostly a country of farmers who struggled to provide for themselves and to supply Britain with food. The potato was the staple crop in Ireland in the eighteenth century. Potatoes are nutritious. The hardy plants grew well in rocky Irish soil. But unfortunately, people stopped planting a variety of types of potatoes and mostly planted only one type. By the early 1840s, half of Ireland depended almost exclusively on that single type of potato for their diet.

This is a fictional story, though it is set outside a real town. The castle and all characters, in particular, are entirely made up. Still, all events of a public nature are based on true events that happened in western Ireland between summer 1846 and spring 1847. That winter was bitterly fierce and punishing, especially after the crop failure. The blight that ruined the potato crops in 1845 and 1846 did not return in 1847. But because there were so few seed potatoes to plant that spring, the harvest of 1847 gave no respite from the famine. Then in 1848 the blight returned.

Conservative estimates put the number of deaths from starvation, exposure to cold, and diseases such as typhus between 1845 and 1852 at around eight hundred thousand. More realistic estimates put it much higher, in the millions, because so many births and deaths in that period went unrecorded. The numbers of people who left Ireland to migrate to the Americas are also very difficult to estimate, because many died en route and their deaths were not recorded. Further, not all who entered Canada or the United States were officially recorded. Many historians estimate that the number of emigrants was at least double the number of those who died in Ireland.

But many people stayed. Some of them simply didn't have the means to leave. But others, like Lorraine and Emmet and Uncle Odran, couldn't bear the idea of leaving their dear Ireland. My hope is to have paid homage to the spirits of all, but particularly those who remained to build a new Ireland.

Go mbeirimíd beo ar an am seo arís. May we all be alive this time next year.

GLOSSARY

Some of these words are Irish words (set in *italics*; anglicized words are in roman type), and others are just unusual words or unusual senses for words you might already know.

be wide: be careful
blasta: tasty
blather: long-winded talk without making sense
bo: cow
bold: naughty
boreen: country path
cottier: peasant farmer working for the tenant farmer
cunning: smart
daft: foolish
dearthâir beag: little brother
dearthâir mór: big brother
dodder: waste time
dosser: lazybones
fooster: waste time by fussing about
gadaí: thief
Galways: the city today called Galway
gaol: jail
give out: complain
haggis: Scottish dish (fully described in the text)
haslet: innards
hurling: Irish field game played with a stick, like field hockey
jumper: sweater

lashed: rained hard
maith: good
manky: filthy
muc: pig
murrain: crop blight
poteen: alcoholic drink made from potatoes
puca: folklore creature
ructions: arguments
saoirse: freedom
shattered: exhausted
sleveen: rogue and trickster
snappers: children
thick: stupid
thruaill: wretched
thurible: metal container for incense

BIBLIOGRAPHY

Donnelly, James S., Jr. *The Great Irish Potato Famine*. Stroud, Gloucestershire: History Press, 2008.

Keegan, Gerald. *Famine Diary: Journey to a New World*. Dublin: Wolfhound Press, 1991. First published in 1895.

Lambert, Henry. *A Memoir of Ireland in 1850, by an Ex-M.P.* Dublin: James McGlashan Publisher, 1851.

Ó Gráda, Cormac. *Black '47 and Beyond: The Great Irish Famine in History, Economy, and Memory*. Princeton, NJ: Princeton University Press, 2000.

Póirtéir, Cathal. *Famine Echoes*. Dublin: Gill & Macmillan Ltd., 1995.

Robinson, Tim. *Connemara: Listening to the Wind*. Dublin: Penguin Ireland, 2006.

———. *Connemara: The Last Pool of Darkness*. Dublin: Penguin Ireland, 2008.

Whelan, Kevin. "The Catholic Parish, the Catholic Chapel and Village Development in Ireland." *Irish Geography* 16, 1 (1983): 1–15.

Woodham-Smith, Cecil. *The Great Hunger: Ireland: 1845–1849*. London: Penguin, 1991. First published in 1962.

There are many sources on the Internet about the famine that give drawings and quotes from newspapers, as well as summaries from printed sources. Search for "Irish potato famine 1845–51."

There are also many books that give an overview of (modern) Irish history, with attention to the famine, including:

Bartlett, Thomas. *Ireland: A History*. Cambridge: Cambridge University Press, 2010.

Beckett, J. C. *The Making of Modern Ireland: 1603-1923*. London: Faber & Faber, 2011. First published in 1981.

Bew, Paul. *Ireland: The Politics of Enmity, 1789-2006*. Oxford: Oxford University Press, 2007.

Comerford, R. V. *Ireland*. London: Hodder Arnold, 2003.

Curtis, Edmund. *A History of Ireland: From the Earliest Times to 1922*. New York: Routledge, 1961. First published in 1936 by Methuen & Co. Ltd.

Foster, R. F. *Modern Ireland: 1600–1972*. London and New York: Penguin, 1990.

Hachey, Thomas E., and Lawrence J. McCaffrey. *The Irish Experience Since 1800: A Concise History*. Fairford, UK: ME Sharpe, 3rd ed., 2010.

Hoppen, K. Theodore. *Ireland Since 1800: Conflict and Conformity*. London: Routledge. 2nd ed., 2013.

Jackson, Alvin. *Home Rule: An Irish History 1800–2000*. Oxford: Oxford University Press, 2003.

———. *Ireland 1798–1998: Politics and War*. Oxford: Blackwell, 1999.

MacDonagh, Oliver, W. F. Mandle, and Pauric Travers, eds. *Irish Culture and Nationalism, 1750–1950*. London: Palgrave Macmillan, 1983.

TIME LINE OF IRELAND TO THE END OF THE FAMINE

Prehistoric times

People inhabited Ireland during the Pleistocene period. During the Stone Age they built megalithic tombs—which were tombs made of enormous stones simply set against one another with no concrete or mortar. More than five hundred of them still exist. One of the most famous is the Newgrange passage tomb, which was built around 3000 BCE.

500 BCE–400 CE

Around 500 BCE the Celts spread from the Alps of central Europe to both the east and the west. When they arrived in Ireland, they settled in—perhaps via force, perhaps not. The Celts had a great advantage in that they knew how to make iron tools. Soon the Celtic way of life prevailed in Ireland. People lived in protected communities as much as they could. Crannogs were forts built on artificial islands in the middle of marshes. Ring forts were farming areas with homes scattered through and earthen walls around the whole thing, sometimes with a timber fence at the top. There were also hill forts and stone forts and subterranean homes. Each settlement had a chieftain, and several settlements were gathered together into minor kingdoms, which were gathered together into primary kingdoms, of which there were a handful. All the various kingdoms of Ireland were first united in the year 379 under Niall Noígíallach.

400 CE–800 CE

The Roman Empire had gained power throughout Europe. While the

Romans never invaded Ireland, they did have considerable influence through trade, and they sent Catholic clergy to Ireland. One priest in particular became a bishop and was later canonized as Saint Patrick, now known as the patron saint of Ireland. Monasteries were built in isolated places, including the tops of rocky mountainous islands off the coastline (a famous one being Skellig Michael). The Catholic faith gradually took hold, and by the end of this period, nearly everyone was Catholic; few pagans remained. Illuminated books were written in Latin, though the people spoke Celtic. These were harsh times worldwide. In 664 a plague swept the country, killing many. Famine was common and severe. While Ireland was united under the descendants of that first king for centuries, the various chieftains had many small wars with one another. Much of the outside world saw Ireland as a wild place.

800 CE–1200 CE

Vikings made small, quick raids on Ireland in their long boats, robbing monasteries, stealing livestock, and kidnapping people to enslave them. Gradually, they moved inland, using rivers as a means to get to new places to raid. Soon the Vikings established camps, long ports, along the coasts. Then inland. Though the Vikings were fought off, they kept coming back. Eventually, Viking camps became permanent towns, including Dublin, Waterford, Cork, Westford, and Limerick. Catholicism and the Irish language (descended from Celtic) prevailed, however, even in predominantly Viking settlements.

Máel Sechnaill mac Máele Ruanaid was the first to hold the title of high king of Ireland in 846, but it wasn't until 1166 that Ireland had its first king that was inaugurated without opposition: Ruaidrí Ua Conchobair (Rory O'Connor). His power didn't last for long, however: Henry II, who held the title of king of England as well as count of Anjou, count of Maine, duke of Normandy, duke of Aquitaine, and count of Nantes, and at various times ruled Brittany, Scotland, and Wales, was involved in battles to overcome Ireland as early as 1169. In 1171, Henry II became supreme ruler of the country.

1200 CE–1600 CE

During these years England had a very mixed influence on Ireland. Irish troops often fought with Anglo-Norman (that is, English and French) troops. Treaties were made, and broken. The country was divided into Irish speakers, who were largely Catholic, and English speakers, who, after the mid-1500s, were largely Protestant. Many monasteries were closed. Laws were enacted forbidding cultural inter-actions between the Irish and English within the country because the Irish were considered barely civilized. Irish poets and musicians, for example, could not go into areas that were predominantly Anglo. Marriage between Catholics and Protestants was illegal. In 1541, King Henry VIII (who had been king of England since 1509) was made king of Ireland by the Irish Parliament, which had been taken over by Anglos and Anglo sympathizers. Nevertheless, the Irish language remained strong and was first put in print in 1571. Irish acts of rebel-lion against English rule became more frequent.

1600 CE–1800 CE

In 1610 settlers from England and Scotland moved to Ireland. This influx led to more unrest. In 1649, Oliver Cromwell, an English par-liamentarian, came to Ireland with English troops to put down Irish rebellions against English rule. In payment for the English soldiers' work, Cromwell gave them Irish land. Many Irish landowners (both those that had participated in the rebellion and those that hadn't) lost land that their families had lived on for centuries. Around 85 percent of the Irish were Catholics, and now Catholics were banned from being members of the Irish Parliament. So the majority was being governed by a minority, largely of foreign origin. England didn't see Ireland as capable of governing itself.

After Cromwell's death, those Irish who had been loyal to England tried to get their land back, but the laws that were passed only led to confusion. This entire period was blighted with fights against the English settlers and the English government, as well as the passing of many anti-Catholic laws and the seizing of more land. By 1709 only about 14 percent of the land in Ireland belonged to Irish Catholics. By 1778 that had shrunk to 5 percent. The Disenfranchising Act of 1727 officially blocked Catholics from voting, although they had been effectively blocked from voting by other penal laws for many years before that. In 1793 the right to vote was re-established, but only a small number of Catholics were, in fact, allowed to vote due to a variety of reasons.

Other blights hit Ireland too: 1725 saw severe famine and sickness due to the potato crop failure. 1740 saw another severe famine. 1782 saw the start of two years of famine.

1801

After a large rebellion, England abolished the Irish Parliament; the Union of Great Britain and Ireland came into law. Ireland would then have representatives in the Parliament of the United Kingdom of Great Britain. Ireland's population comprised more than 40 percent of the United Kingdom, yet the Irish held only 105 of the 658 seats in the Parliament at Westminster, England. There were food shortages throughout Ireland. The British government did not seem terribly concerned. The attitude that the Irish were substandard people—an attitude that went back centuries—persisted.

1803

Robert Emmet led a rising of the Irish against the English. He was executed for treason.

The potato crop failed. There was famine and an outbreak of typhus.

1821

The United Kingdom took the first national census of Ireland and there were official inquiries into the issue of poverty there. Many British were becoming alarmed at a situation they had not recognized.

1829

A Relief Act was passed; now Catholics could be members of parliament and hold office.

1833

A royal commission carried out a three-year survey to study the situation of the poor in Ireland. The Irish were clearly not thriving under British rule. Many were encouraged to emigrate. Landlords were encouraged to employ more Irish. Thomas Malthus, a famous English economist of the time, wrote that the poor of Ireland were useless and "should be swept from the soil" so that the resources of that land could go unhindered to Britain.

1838

After years of discussing the pervasive poverty of the Irish and their need for "character" to pull them out of that poverty, and years of ineffective attempts to ameliorate the situation, the British passed the Irish Poor Law Act. It established workhouses for paupers. There was no guarantee of relief; access to the workhouses depended on how many spaces were available. The burden of maintaining a workhouse fell on the people local to that workhouse—a system that was intended to get landlords involved in raising the overall economic state of the people.

1839

Poverty was at an all-time high in the south and west of Ireland. But the Poor Law commissioners of the British government would not allow government funding to help out.

1840

Nearly half the population of Ireland ate potatoes as the foundation of their nutrition. Few ate grains or meat regularly. At the same time, Ireland produced tons of grains and livestock that were exported by the landlords to increase their own wealth. Britain was fed by those grains and livestock.

1845

There were 118 workhouses in Ireland. Only one third of them kept fever patients separate from others. That was the situation when the potato blight hit—an already weakened and impoverished population was struck with a calamity that would have brought the strongest to their knees. In August a fungus-like organism that had been brought to Belgium in a cargo of seed potatoes reached England and spread. It was in Ireland in September. Ireland had suffered many famines, but this was the worst of them all. Half the potato crop was ruined by the fungus-like organism. There were rumors among the English that the Irish were "exaggerating" how bad the situation was. So the English landlords continued to export grains and livestock from Ireland to England—thinking that the Irish didn't really need that food. The English also believed that Ireland would get through it somehow because Ireland had always managed to get through past blights. But this time famine was widespread.

1846

Ireland was sick. The starving population was struck with influenza, jaundice, and small pox. It killed children, women, men, everyone. Diarrhea and dysentery were at epidemic levels from eating rotten potatoes. In February, Indian corn was brought to Ireland to feed those in the poorhouses and sell to those still in their homes. The rationale was that this was cheaper than feeding the Irish the grains that they had grown themselves. But there weren't enough mills in Ireland to grind that corn down into edible flour. So people still kept getting sick and starving to death. By March there were more than forty-seven thousand inmates in Irish workhouses. Poor people now sought work day by day with the government public works. In July public works employed an average of seventy-one thousand workers daily. By August it was clear the blight had returned. Starvation was insistent. People flocked to the workhouses. By Christmas more than 50 percent of workhouses were full to capacity. The price of whatever grain there was skyrocketed. The Irish seemed doomed. Death was a daily occurrence in town after town.

1847

Ireland was in crisis. In January the British government finally opened soup kitchens. But it was too late. Each week twenty-seven hundred people were dying in workhouses. That's more than ten thousand a month! By February nearly all Ireland's workhouses were full. In March the Choctaw Nation of North America raised $170 for relief of Irish famine victims—a very high sum at that time. Other groups in America also sent money, including the city of Philadelphia. Still, the British, who were close enough to see the decimation of the people, held back on aid. Many British voices called the Irish lazy and reckless and blamed their situation on their lack of moral character. In April all public works jobs ended, and the task of feeding the poor fell solely on the soup kitchens. Between January and April ninety thousand Irish emigrated from Ireland to Liverpool. In May a mob of the poor in County Cork threatened to smash the soup kitchens because the defective food served there made them sick with a disease similar to "sea scurvy." They demanded money or bread. Cork alone had around twenty thousand paupers who had come into town from the countryside. Many people bought guns. They were fed up with seeing death all around them while the landlords in Ireland and the general populace in Britain were still thriving. But not all the British turned a blind eye; private donations from Britain poured in. The Church of England said help was needed urgently. Emigration to Canada was high, but the ships were riddled with fever and many died on board. At home in Ireland, fever was epidemic. In July the government decided to let the food depots run out. Relief efforts ended. Typhus raged. Nuns, clergymen, and doctors who cared for the sick were sick now as well. By August, beggars were everywhere. Landowners were supposed to take responsibility—and they did it by trying to force the Irish to emigrate. If a small landowner turned over land to another, then the receiving landlord had to pay two thirds of the emigration costs of the seller. The government would pay the rest. But so few people owned any land that hardly any Irish were helped by this. Begging was outlawed, so more people did it in hopes of being sent to prison, where they would be fed. Many acts were passed to supply relief; nothing was successful. In August many soup kitchens in the east and midlands were closed. The people had nothing to eat but what they could forage. The rest of the soup kitchens were closed by October. Then, amazingly, there was no blight in fall 1847. But the planting in the spring had been so limited that the harvest was still small and there was still severe food shortage after that harvest. Dysentery and scurvy kept increasing. Landlords evicted workers who were useless. Many homeless people were afraid to go into the workhouses because of the diseases festering there. Britain was having its own economic problems now, with an industrial depression and a run on the banks. So sentiment against spending money on Irish relief grew. People called the Irish "ungrateful and lawless."

1848

All through that winter the workhouses were full, and fever raged through the emaciated people living in them. By May one million people daily were getting relief from the Poor Law, mostly through workhouses. Landlords continued to evict tenants. In June a ship of orphaned Irish girls, aged fourteen to eighteen, was sent by the British to Australia, where the girls found employment. Most were Protestant girls. And only those who could do needlework and washing were sent, which ruled out most girls from the west, where poverty was the cruelest. People were still dying in the thousands. Then the worst happened: That summer the blight was back again. And it was as bad as it had been in autumn of 1846—it was the worst blight all over again. Famine persisted. Thousands of new applicants applied to the workhouses every day. In December cholera hit many. Tens of thousands died.

1849

The British debated the fate of Ireland while cholera kept killing thousands. In April the Poor Law Commissioners ran out of money because debates kept the government from approving more. Little bits were approved here and there, but not enough. But by summer the cholera epidemic had ended at least. And, finally, that summer saw a healthy crop with a good harvest in the fall. But so many were sick, homeless, and out of work that relief was still needed. And many more children had been orphaned by now. So the government put more orphans on ships and sent them elsewhere.

1850

Many Irish emigrated to Liverpool, England, where they were stuffed into lodging houses at costs higher than the English had been paying. The conditions were squalid and those who were not already ill often wound up ill. Back in Ireland people were slowly gathering strength. Come autumn, there was a good harvest, with blight only here and there. Ireland was finally pulling out of the cycle of death.

1851

A census showed a drop in population of more than one and a half million people during the preceding decade. No one knows how many people were born and died during that decade without their lives ever being counted in this figure. Conservative estimates say that around a million people died and even more emigrated. That would mean at least one quarter of the population was either dead or living in another country at the end of the famine. The west of Ireland—in counties like the one in this story—was the hardest hit in terms of both deaths and emigration.

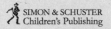